THE SETUP

THE SETUP

TB MARKINSON

OTHER TB MARKINSON BOOKS

A Woman Lost Series
The Miracle Girl Series
Girl Love Happens Series
Reservations of the Heart
A Shot at Love
One Golden Summer

Copyright © 2020 T. B. Markinson

Published by T. B. Markinson

Cover Design by Victoria Cooper

Edited by Kelly Hashway

This book is copyrighted and licensed for your personal enjoyment only. All rights reserved. No part of this publication may be reproduced, stored in a retrieval system, or transmitted in any forms or by any means without the prior permission of the copyright owner. The moral rights of the authors have been asserted.

This book is a work of fiction. Names, characters, businesses, places, events, and incidents are the product of the authors' imagination or are used fictitiously. Any resemblance to actual persons, living or dead, events, or locales is entirely coincidental.

A NOTE ABOUT THE SETUP

Thanks so much for purchasing *The Setup*. I really appreciate your support, and I hope you enjoy the story.

When I started 2020, this novella wasn't on my writing schedule. In fact, the story hadn't entered my mind at all. When things started getting out of hand in March, I was in London. For a few days, I thought I'd get stuck in Britain to ride out the pandemic.

Luckily, I made it back to Boston, but after roughly ten days, I started getting sick. I have no idea what illness struck me down, but whatever it was, it was a doozy. The next few months became a roller coaster of feeling okay and not doing well at all.

A NOTE ABOUT THE SETUP

When it came time for me to write fresh words, I didn't have it in me to pen the angsty novel that was originally on my schedule. I wanted something lighthearted and set in a place seeped with happy memories. That's what London is for me. My happy place.

The reason I didn't want to get stuck there was my loved ones were in the US, and enduring the pandemic without the better half wasn't high on my list of how to survive a once-in-a-lifetime event. But I wanted to return to London even if it was only via writing.

The Setup is the result, and I hope you enjoy reading it as much as I liked writing it.

LET'S KEEP IN TOUCH

One of the best parts of publishing is getting to know *you* the reader, and my favorite method of keeping in touch is via my newsletter.

I share about my life, upcoming new releases, promotions, and giveaways.

And, I give away two e-books to two newsletter subscribers every month. The winners will be able to choose from my backlist or an upcoming release.

I love giving back to you, which is why if you join my newsletter, I'll send you a free e-copy of *A Woman Lost*, book 1 of the A Woman Lost series, and bonus chapters you can't get anywhere else.

If you want to keep in touch, sign up here: http://eepurl.com/dtzNv1

CHAPTER ONE

The sound of a truck backing up, followed by a man shouting, tore me from a deep sleep. Sitting up, I rubbed my eyes, cursing the rude welcome to the start of my new life in a foreign land. Thoughts swished around in my head, due to not getting my required eight hours after going to bed at a quarter after midnight. The alarm I'd set for 8:15 hadn't gone off yet.

Blinking, I took in the state of chaos in my new apartment—no, they say *flat* here—and released an anguished sigh. Half-empty boxes, brown wrapping paper, and what little belongings I'd brought seemed to be mocking me. To make matters worse, while I had coffee grinds, I hadn't purchased a new coffee maker yet. The one in the furnished apartment didn't pass my sniff test, and there was no way I'd use something that had a strange film in the reservoir tank. I'd heard about the hard water in London, but it wasn't until I saw what it could do that I understood the meaning.

Stretching my arms overhead, I contemplated curling back under the covers, and ditching my plans for the day. Me without a cup of joe first thing spelled disaster of epic proportions, and did the world need to experience that firsthand?

The yelling outside intensified, and I clambered out of bed to peer through the window, looking up to spy the cause of the commotion, but from the basement vantage point, I could only see the lower half of people's legs and the occasional face of a dog sniffing the pavement.

I could make out some of the words: *Arsehole, blighter, git, bloody hell, duffer, codger,* and some others that seemed even more insulting. I struggled deciphering how many were involved in the argument, since at least one voice sounded far away. Did this qualify as sport in this country?

The alarm on my phone trilled, but I couldn't find it.

Finally, I discovered it under my pillow. I silenced the alarm and tossed the phone back onto the murphy bed. I'd expected to be stiff after sleeping on only a mattress, but my landlord had said he invested in the top-of-the-line murphy beds, and the tarp-like springs were superior to proper box springs. In the moment, I hadn't believed him, but the bathroom in this place was clean, so I thought the trade-off would be an unbearable mattress. That wasn't the case yet, and fingers crossed it didn't become an issue.

I waded through the stacks of boxes, heading for the bathroom on the other side of the double doors of the main area.

After battling the thin shower curtain, which kept clinging to my wet body (I mentally added a weighted shower curtain to my shopping list), I ran a hand through my shoulder-length hair in a pathetic attempt to style it. I still hadn't located the box with my hair styling products, and I needed to buy a blow-dryer because my American one didn't have the right plug.

Only forty minutes into my first day of waking up in London, and I already needed to track down a coffee maker, hair dryer, and a non-grabby shower curtain. I jotted down the items in my notes app before hurriedly tossing on cut-off jean shorts and a V-neck shirt that was entirely too wrinkled but readily available. Then I located my large shoulder bag, which was under a pile of clothes on a chair, and locked up my flat.

I was impressed with myself, considering I'd only been on the island less than twenty-four hours and I was already out for an adventure. On paper, I sounded pretty boring. A twenty-seven-year-old accountant from Denver, Colorado. But what many didn't bother to see was my zest for life, including experiences big and small. When I learned about my London transfer, I promised myself I wouldn't waste a second of exploring, and I was off to a stellar start.

As I closed the gate at the top of the stairs, the horrendous metal-on-metal squeal caused me to wince. I checked the right pocket of my shorts to ensure I had my key. I had a fear of locking myself out after I did exactly that with my first apartment back in college. My fingers wrapped around the long, gangly key, so unlike the ones we have in America. The fact that everything was different here brought a satisfied smile to my face.

"Rory!"

I whipped around to my landlord, an older white-haired gentleman sporting a three-piece suit that seemed trendy solely because none of the colors went together. Was that a British thing or his particular sense of fashion?

"Good morning, Nigel."

He held one of the black balusters on the railing, his grizzled and spotted hand shaking. "I hope you had a peaceful night's rest."

I started to say yes, but he barreled on. "I had to shout at a lorry driver for parking on the pavement. He doesn't care if he cracks it. Why would he? He doesn't have to pay for upkeep in this neighborhood." As he spoke, visible drops of spittle sprayed the air, forcing me to take a step back. "This country is falling apart. Too many immigrants, but I'll have the last laugh.

Mark my words." His sweet smile and charming British accent jarred with the remarks.

I gawked at my landlord, wondering if he'd forgotten I was American, which classified me as an immigrant. I had the work visa to prove it. Given my company was paying my rent for two years, he didn't see me as part of the problem but as a source for his retirement fund. He'd joked about it when I flew out the previous month for a whirlwind apartment shopping frenzy, leaving me feeling like I never had time to visit interesting places, only one unacceptable apartment after another until I found this one, which was absurdly small, but the newly painted walls, clean kitchen, and mold-free bathroom sold me. After some of the places I'd seen, my list of must-haves dwindled to those items, hence why I was able to overlook the murphy bed.

He made his way around me on the sidewalk to unlock his antique shop situated above my flat. He owned the whole building, which consisted of four flats, including the one at the top where he lived. At first, the thought of having the landlord on the premises seemed quaint, but after his immigrant comment, I wondered if it was going to cause problems.

No matter. I was running late, something I loathed.

"I hate to dash, but I'm meeting a friend for breakfast."

He nodded, tapping his umbrella on the ground. "Enjoy the weather while it lasts."

We both looked up to the brilliant blue sky.

"Will do." I tucked my head down and walked briskly past the dry cleaners and Italian restaurant, the staff setting out tables and chairs on a small tiled patio. I imagined they'd be hopping for lunch and dinner on this beautiful August day.

On Bayswater Road, across the street from the Italian Fountains entrance of Kensington Gardens, I hung a right, heading toward the Notting Hill Gate Tube Entrance. According to the directions on my phone, it was a straight shot on this road, and it'd take twenty-five minutes. I had twenty, so I booked it.

It was ten minutes past nine on a Saturday, so the sidewalk wasn't packed. A man wearing a blue shirt and yellow vest was clutching a handful of tour bus pamphlets. He tried to hook me with his spiel, but I uttered "no thanks" and continued on my way.

Outside one of the corner pubs, a scraggly man spraying the sidewalk with a hose, a hand-rolled cigarette in his mouth, shut off the water to let me pass. Again, I mumbled a thanks and wished him a good day.

He nodded, getting back to cleaning.

A red double-decker bus rumbled by, bringing an *I live in London* smile to my lips. I passed a red phone booth. Red postbox. My eyes swept the fronts of businesses on the street, landing on Café Diana. I squinted, looking through the windows to see countless photos of the princess. This truly hammered home my reality.

I was in London, a place I'd always wanted to live since watching *Bedknobs and Broomsticks* when I was all of five years old. When my company asked for volunteers to move abroad, the adventurer inside me couldn't toss my name into the hat quickly enough. The options on the table were London, Tokyo, and Hong Kong, and I wouldn't get a choice. All of the places would make a great base for me to achieve one of my childhood dreams: to see the world. My grandfather, who fought in Africa in World War II, had given me a globe for Christmas one year—I think I was six or seven—and I still loved to spin it and stop on a country. When I was a kid, I'd race to our encyclopedia set to research the place my finger landed. Now, I pulled up a wiki page on my phone.

At first, it looked as if I was heading to Hong Kong, but at the last minute, those offices were put on the back burner, and the powers that be decided London would be my new home. It was exciting and terrifying that I didn't actually have a say, like being in the military, minus the uniform and ungodly wake-up calls.

Eight months later, I stood outside the Notting Hill Gate tube stop. How bloody fantastic was my life? I wanted to tell everyone the great news. That I had made it. Not only to London, but to the adventurer stage of my life. But all the faces of those around me didn't pay me the time of day.

A man bumped into my shoulder, snapping me out of my trance. I peered around at my surroundings but couldn't recall the directions, so I consulted my phone to see which side street to turn onto for the café.

Back on track, I arrived outside of the café at thirty-one minutes past nine. Not bad, considering the chaotic morning. Now it was time for coffee, because I wasn't fit for civilized society until after at least one cup, preferably two.

The *I fucking live in London* thoughts could only power me so far. Getting into the three-customers-deep line, my eyes scanned the board hanging on the wall behind the register. A family of four brushed past me, angry French words assaulting my ears, but I wasn't the source of the frustration, judging by the fussy toddler, exasperated mother, red-faced father, and the sibling who clearly already had enough of family-bonding time. Their day out in London didn't seem to have the same hope as mine.

I stepped up to the register. "May I please have an Americano." I quickly added, "For here."

After placing my order, I glanced around and seized on two important pieces of information. Only one table was available, and the staff didn't bring items to customers. So, I placed my bag over one of the chairs, claiming my space. I'd learned this trait after working in the financial district of Boston. One wasted second could cost so much.

An employee caught my eye, and I moved forward to retrieve the glass mug placed on a saucer.

"Thank you," I said and turned around, nearly taking out the person behind me, the tall glass wobbling. I reached for it before it toppled, exclaiming, "Whoa! Steady!"

"Excuse me? You bumped into me."

Settling the drink, my eyes moved from the person's shoes, up dark fitting jeans, and continued a long way until I met brilliant blue eyes. "I wasn't yelling at you but at the coffee in an attempt to convince it not to spill."

"You were talking to your coffee?" Her delightful accent and expression remained stoic, perhaps in an attempt to mask her annoyance.

"Yes. Sorry. I'll get out of your way."

The woman stood to the side.

With my head tucked down for the second time this morning, I took the five steps to safety, wishing I hadn't bothered to get out of bed and rush to meet my friend who still hadn't arrived yet.

Taking a seat, I checked my phone and discovered a text saying: *Be there soon!*

So far, my interactions with Brits in London had been awkward at best.

The woman from the confrontation waited for her beverage, allowing me to sneak glances at her long, silky blonde tresses and curves. Her *first thing in the morning* outfit put my faded jean shorts and Denver Broncos T-shirt to shame. Was her outfit an indication of how Europeans dressed on the weekend? I thought Nigel was an outlier due to his age, but everything this woman wore looked like freshly purchased designer clothes that cost a pretty penny. If that was the case, I needed to add shopping to my urgent to-do list to avoid being seen as a sloppy American tourist. While I was American, I wasn't a tourist. That thought returned the smile to my lips.

She retrieved her drink and turned around, her eyes panning the available tables, but the one and only space was near me, and she seemed intent on not looking in my direction.

I couldn't blame the woman, considering I nearly splattered her top-shelf outfit with coffee.

Her gaze went to the front again, still hopeful to find a place, but no one seemed to be near clearing out.

"There's a seat here," I called, hoping it wasn't overly American or pushy. According to my UK coworkers in the Boston office, it was a common American trait everyone in the world despised.

She met my gaze, a look of defeat clouding those startling blue eyes. Nodding—was she summoning courage?—she accepted the offer.

I hopped to my feet. "The tables can be separated if you want your own space."

Relief washed over her.

"Set your drink on my table. No need to tempt fate twice in five minutes." I let out a nervous laugh, sounding a bit like what I imagined an excited hyena puppy emitted when playing with litter mates. Was I determined to make an ass or *arse* out of myself?

After she placed her drink down, we pulled the tables a few inches apart, which didn't give the woman much buffer room from me, the American barbarian, but it was the best I could do, and it appeased my need to make the coffee snafu right.

Much to my surprise, the woman took the chair next to me. Perhaps she wanted to look out the window to observe the hurly-burly as people made their way to Portobello for the Saturday antique fair. Or quite possibly, she only wanted me in her peripheral vision.

Again, I couldn't blame her. Instead of focusing on the woman, which wasn't easy given her beauty, I turned my brain to food. Starving, I wanted a stack of pancakes, dripping with maple syrup, and a side of extra crispy bacon. I could almost taste it.

My stomach grumbled.

Embarrassed, I shifted in my seat, while coughing into my shoulder in a terrible attempt to mask my stomach screaming for food.

The woman seemed to sneak a peek at me but didn't make a sound or move.

Jane entered the café. Her hair was dyed pink, and

she was wearing a flowing skirt and blouse like she was an extra in *Fiddler on the Roof*. She grinned and waved.

I waved back.

So did the woman but with much less enthusiasm.

What the…?

Jane approached. "Oh good, you two have met."

CHAPTER TWO

"What?" I opened and closed my mouth. "Met who? You?" I pointed at her.

Jane laughed, brushing my arms to the side and giving me a hug. "We met years ago. Don't you remember?"

After I sat back down, I said, "Yes, I do. Don't you remember our yearly trips to the Big Apple, or did you get hit in the head or something on your way here? Is that why you're running late?" I moved my head to the left and then right, followed by up and down, trying to see if there were any marks or other signs of trauma.

Jane shook her head, still laughing. Then, she walked around my chair and hugged the blonde.

My jaw nearly hit the floor. It would have been helpful to know a third person was joining us for coffee. It probably wouldn't have changed the earlier near-coffee disaster, and there had been no indication the blonde was the third wheel. Still, if I'd known it wasn't going to be just Jane and me, I may have selected a different outfit. Jane was used to my devotion to the Broncos, an NFL team that promised disappointment with glimmers of a playoff run. I was a fan of hope.

Taking the seat across from me, Jane said in a TV announcer way, "Rory Price, I'd like you to meet Imogen Wright."

I turned to the blonde. "Oh, hi."

Imogen nodded, but her bunched eyebrows indicated she was as befuddled by the circumstances as I was.

"I need coffee. Can I get you two anything? Rory, you don't have food. You always need food." Jane spoke rapidly, one of the outcomes of managing theater productions in the past, which required her to juggle ten tasks per minute, without slowing down to assess how things were going wrong. Like this coffee date.

She was spot-on about my hunger, though, and I pushed aside my annoyance to check out the options. "Flapjacks, please."

"Imogen?" Jane arched one of her dark eyebrows.

The woman shook her head, still not uttering a word, which I understood on one level given the ambush, but it didn't bode well for a peaceful coffee.

Jane got in line, while I looked to Imogen, my mind going completely blank. Finally, it latched on to some words. "How do you know Jane? She's one of my exes."

Damn, I wished I could retract the last part, which was TMI. There was no reason why this person needed to know I'd slept with Jane. The situation was already awkward, and I cranked it up a level closer to unbearable.

"University." She avoided eye contact, her eyes bouncing on every possible person and surface, never resting but not getting anywhere near me.

Couple my blunder with her one-word answer, and I had the urge to stand up and say, "This, ladies and gentlemen, is how not to make a first impression. Can you point out where I went wrong? Let's learn from this together."

My warm fuzzy feelings about being in Britain started to dim. Even in a new country, awkward social situations were an inescapable ingredient in my life. It was always disappointing when my imagined self, who dazzled a beautiful woman with witty banter, fizzled under the harsh light of reality. Was I destined to always be the boring accountant no one noticed for the right reasons?

Clearly, this woman, who piqued my interest, didn't want anything to do with me. Was it simply due to the coffee debacle, or was there another underlying reason? My landlord's comment about immigrants popped into my mind, and once again, I rued my T-shirt choice and lack of hair dryer. Had my brown curls turned into frizz?

I also regretted my decision of getting out of bed to meet Jane on my first full day since hopping the pond. When Jane had extended the invite, I was ecstatic. Having someone I knew in my new city was a comfort.

Until she'd tossed me headfirst into the deep end of the awkward pool. Really, I didn't need help in that department.

Jane returned with a coffee and fruit tart for her, and she placed a plate down in front of me.

"What's this?" I poked one of the items in question.

"Your flapjacks, silly. That's what you wanted, right?"

"Oh, yes, of course. Sorry, the caffeine hasn't kicked in." I tried to wipe away my disappointment upon receiving two oatmeal bars that looked nothing like American pancakes. Lesson one of London life.

"What have you two been talking about?" Jane popped a blueberry into her mouth.

Absolutely nothing, but I didn't want to toss Imogen under the bus. "Oh, how you two went to school together."

"Until I dropped out." Jane sipped her coffee, still not picking up on the fact that her friend wanted nothing to do with me.

"Is that right?" I looked to Imogen and then Jane.

"Isn't that interesting? Not that you quit. That's none of my beeswax."

Jane's brow furrowed, probably because I had already known this detail. Why wasn't my brain properly functioning?

Imogen stood. "I need to use the loo."

I smiled and bobbed my head like a fool, as if going to the bathroom was as exciting as getting onto a roller coaster. I'm surprised I didn't follow my thought with, "Weee!" which would be funny if she got it, but she was already gone.

I leaned over the table and whispered, "What are you up to?"

Jane swallowed a bite. "Eating a tart?"

"Don't play innocent with me." I jabbed a finger in the air.

She dropped her eyes, but her lips curled into a mischievous smile. Jane was the type who loved improv, thinking most things in life should be acted out as if on the stage. That was her comfortable place, and she believed all of us would benefit from conquering the fear of making an ass out of oneself.

"I thought we were spending the day together." I didn't attempt to avoid sounding like a petulant child.

"We are." She bounced in her seat, brimming with excitement. It was nauseating, really.

"What about Imogen?"

"What about her?" Jane leveled her shoulders, trying to look innocent.

"Why is she here? She hates me."

"She doesn't even know you, so that seems a bit extreme. Even for you."

"What do you mean by that?"

Jane placed a hand on my arm. "What's wrong with you today? Are you jet-lagged or something?"

I was something but couldn't put my finger on what. Not that I had time, because Imogen reappeared, looking like someone had tossed her into a shark tank minus any protective gear.

After she retook her seat, Jane said, "Rory says you hate her. Is that true?"

I stared daggers at Jane.

Imogen shifted in her seat, her eyes meeting Jane, and the unspoken message was loud and clear. It could only be described as: *first chance I get, I'm going to tell you exactly what I think*.

Jane, though, didn't feel ill at ease at all. Instead, her shoulders softened, and she heartily laughed. "You two are so uptight. It's a beautiful summer day. Don't be this way. Not when two of my good friends have finally met."

Funny, because I'd never heard of Imogen before.

Jane pressed on. "Rory and I met when we were both camp counselors in the Berkshires. We dated."

"For a week, I think," I clarified in a tone I hoped made it clear we'd been mismatched and only hooked up because we were the only lesbians at the camp. Perhaps, I wanted Imogen to know Jane wasn't my ideal woman. I hadn't figured out who or what I wanted in life, but the flighty Jane wasn't it.

"Yes, you're right. Sometimes it's best to realize that early and switch gears to friendship. Like Imogen and I did."

"You two dated?" I asked, flabbergasted. Another useful tidbit that could have prevented me from insinuating Jane wasn't my type. Was she Imogen's? Had I accidentally insulted Imogen's taste in women?

"Yes." Jane drained her espresso and stood. "I need another. Anyone else?"

I nodded, while Imogen shook her head.

Jane left after asking me what I wanted. For the second time in as many minutes or so, it seemed she left me alone with the gorgeous blonde.

"I can't believe her," I said, shredding a paper napkin in my hands.

"She's in a class of her own."

"Perfectly put." I turned in my seat. "Imagine her arranging two of her exes. Well, Jane and I were more of a fling." *Stay on point, Rory.* "The nerve of her arranging for us to meet and not letting either one of us know. You didn't know, did you?"

Imogen shook her head, her gaze on me, sending a warm sensation through my body. Those blues sparkled brighter than any gem I'd seen.

"What game is she playing?" I pondered aloud.

"The dating one, I imagine."

Imogen's accent was beyond charming. I'd chalked

up my brief fling with Jane to wanting to experience having a flighty, full-of-life woman in my life. As it turned out, it had been beyond stressful. But had it actually been the British accent that pulled me in? Did I have a type? If Imogen had a type, it wasn't me, given I was nothing like Jane, aside from being a female. No charming accent. Not a *bigger than life* personality. My mousy-brown curls paled to Jane's pink do.

I was the opposite in almost every regard. I grew up in Colorado, a place not known for sexy American accents. In fact, whenever I took a quiz to determine what type of accent I had, the results always came back as not having a distinguishable one. Unlike New Yorkers, Bostonians, Texans, the American South, or other regions with well-known speech patterns. Bland—that was the word to describe my Americanness. Add being an accountant on top of that, and well, I was dead in the water for the likes of Imogen.

My mind raced for an escape route. I'd already denied being jet-lagged, so that option was out. Jane was my only friend in the city. Unfortunately, she knew the movers had arrived yesterday, so I couldn't claim that. But I did have unpacking to do. Not a lot, but Jane didn't know that. Could I use that as my escape hatch? Simply say I needed to cut the day short after drinking my second coffee? Would that be too obvious and offend Imogen? She hadn't been super friendly, but the Coloradoan in me never wanted even a whiff of slighting someone.

"How long are you visiting?" Imogen asked.

"Uh..." Flustered by her pursuing a conversation thread, I had a difficult time forming words. I mentioned I'm awkward, right? "I'm not visiting, actually. My company transferred me here."

There was a flicker in her eyes. "What do you think so far?"

"This is my first time leaving my apartment—I mean flat—and so far, I find London charming. The people seem nice." Damn. Why did I toss that in? Would she think I was purposefully being a jerk instead of not knowing how to handle the situation? "Are you from here? I mean, London. Not Britain."

Jesus, Rory!

"Yep. I grew up near here but spent a few years south of the river in Tooting—"

"Tooting! That sounds funny. Are you pulling my leg, or is that really a place?" I mentally palm-slapped my forehead.

This brought a smile to her face, the first one, and oh, my. She had a lovely smile. "It is."

Her accent tickled my eardrums in such a pleasurable way, and I had to force myself not to say those words, knowing it'd come out oh so wrong. I searched my brain for something else to latch onto.

"What's Tooting known for?" *Please don't say flatulence.*

"It's called the land of the curry mile."

"I love curry!" At least my excitement was real.

"You'll have to check it out, then. I can recommend some places. Brick Lane also has decent curry."

"Brick Lane." I opened my notes app on my phone and jotted down both places. "I'm hoping to see *all* of London."

Imogen laughed. "I've been living here all my life, and I feel like I've barely cracked the surface. Where's your flat?"

"In Bayswater. One of the side streets right across from the Italian Fountain entrance of Kensington Gardens, which I haven't even had a chance to visit yet. I'm fresh off the boat." I cringed after blurting that part, knowing the racist connotations, which hadn't been my purpose. Merely an attempt at a lame joke. Quickly, I added, "I mean, I flew in yesterday but haven't explored yet."

"And, Portobello Road is your first choice?" She arched one eyebrow.

"Yes." The temperature in my face kicked up to embarrassment level. "As a kid, I loved the movie *Bedknobs and Broomsticks*."

Her smile was kind, but she seemed at a loss for words.

I sought out Jane, who still waited to the side for the drinks. The noise level of the café had noticeably risen, given the uptick of people waiting for service was a sign the tourists were descending like locusts.

Imogen's eyes also panned the interior of the café,

but judging by her stiffening shoulders, she didn't seem thrilled by the turn of events.

"Do you live nearby? Or are you still in Toot-ing?" I asked, unfortunately emphasizing the last word by over enunciating both syllables.

"I'm in Earl's Court, now. It's not far from here."

"Do you like Portobello Road?"

"I like this neighborhood, but I've never been on a weekend when it's crowded."

I blinked. "How is that possible?"

"I'm not a tourist."

CHAPTER THREE

Jane returned with my coffee, dashing back to grab hers, which the barista had set down. The silence between Imogen and me had descended yet again. Try as I might, I couldn't get a decent read on her. Was she terribly shy and geeky, which I could totally relate to? Had she had a bad night and was taking it out on the world? Who among us hadn't committed that sin? Or was she simply a stone-cold bitch? Hopefully, I never fell into this category. I really didn't get that vibe from her, leaving me to think it was either option one or two.

Jane resettled into her seat, fluffing her pink hair in a movie-star way, and asked, "What'd I miss?"

Imogen sipped her coffee, her eyes darting to the far side of the café, where a table of four excitedly chatted in a language I didn't recognize. Portuguese, perhaps?

I struggled for how to describe the situation to myself, let alone to Jane, who was a notorious busybody. I settled for "Imogen used to live in a place called Tooting. Isn't that a hoot?"

Honestly, I wouldn't have been surprised if I started to hoot like an owl or worse toot. I wasn't always this awkward, but it tended to involve being around a beautiful woman, hence why my single days far outnumbered my relationship ones. Why couldn't I be a lady-killer for one day in my life? Hell, I'd settled for someone who was normal and could discuss politics or tennis with Imogen. Wasn't that big here with Wimbledon?

"Tell me something I don't know." Jane looked to me, then to Imogen, and then back at me. Could she not see how her plan was unraveling before her very eyes?

Imogen reached into a pocket and pulled out her phone. "Excuse me."

The phone hadn't made any noise, so I suspected she was faking a call. Another thing I could relate to. I didn't want to be around me, either.

Imogen strode outside.

I crossed my arms and leveled my eyes on Jane. "Explain yourself."

"Explain what?" Jane met my steely glare with innocence, and I had to hand it to her. She was pretty convincing, but I wasn't going to cave on this.

"You've told me stories of your legendary matchmaking skills, but I've never been one of your victims until now."

"Victim!" Jane heartily laughed.

"Did it ever cross your mind that setting up two of your exes was a bad—no, absolutely horrendous idea?" I sliced two hands in the air.

"Oh, please. I didn't date either of you long enough to merit a full-fledged ex badge."

"You know you're only proving my point, not yours." I gave her the bitchiest look I could conjure up, which wasn't all that bad because I was much too nice. Something I heard a lot from friends dissecting my failed attempts at dating. Even in the lesbian world, the nice ones ended up alone.

"Can you give her a chance?"

"Why should I bother? She's clearly uncomfortable with the situation. I can't blame her for that. Also, I'm only here on a two-year visa. Dating or a relationship isn't on my list for my time here. Not at all!" I tapped on the screen of my phone, even though my actual to-do list wasn't showing.

Jane started to protest, but I raised a hand in the air. "I have two goals while in London: advance my career and enjoy London. Those are it."

"Where's the fun in either?" Jane joggled her hands in an exaggerated motion.

"The career goal really isn't an option now that I'm nearing thirty. I've found having a roof over my head and food on my table are sorta vital components of being an adult. As for the other"—I leaned over the table—"I'm living in the city I've always dreamed of living in. That excitement alone will keep me pleasantly occupied for the next twenty-four months and curb the impulse of inviting women trouble into my life."

"As far as I'm concerned, you've never had female problems."

"I didn't until you came along." I pierced her gaze with a steely one of my own, not wanting to share the dearth of my experience with women, unless ending up being the bestie counted, which Jane was already familiar with.

"I told you we didn't date long enough for that."

"I wasn't talking about us." I pointed to Imogen's empty chair. "This has been an utter fail, and I'm mad you inflicted it on me and Imogen."

"You haven't given it a chance!"

"I can't even wrap my head around why you think this is a good idea. When you invited me, I thought we'd be spending time catching up. It's been months since our last trip together. I never thought today would be a setup. Never in a million years. I just got to London—"

"We are spending time together!" she butted in. "I know you two will like each other. I have great taste in women."

"Then why aren't you dating her?"

"Because she's not right for me."

"She's not right for me, either." I jerked my head to the woman pacing on the sidewalk, phone to her ear. "If you haven't noticed, she's excused herself twice in the span of ten minutes. Probably not even that long."

"Stop looking for every reason to shut down something before giving it a chance. I'm not saying you have to date her, but you're new to London. She's a good egg and has been an excellent friend to me. It doesn't hurt to have friends."

"Can we talk about something else?"

"Sure. What?"

"I'm asking locals about their must-do recommendations in London. What are yours?" I steepled my fingers.

She squinted one eye, staring at the ceiling. "Does it have to be in London? I try to escape the city whenever I get the chance."

"Okay, what's your must do in general?"

"Shopping in Paris."

"Paris, France?" I held my index finger over my phone, not wanting to add that to my *things to do in Britain* list. It was like Jane was dead set on chucking a wrench into any and all of my plans simply for the sake of fucking with me. I'd known she was a free spirit, but I didn't know she was the devil incarnate.

"Yes." She bobbed her head with certainty.

I sighed in frustration. "You know you're recommending I leave the country I want to explore."

"It's only the UK. There's nothing special about it."

She hefted a shoulder and sipped her drink. "We should book a weekend trip to Paris. Not during the summer, though. Too many tourists. They ruin everything."

It was the third time this morning it'd either been insinuated or outright said aloud tourists and/or foreigners sucked. I scrunched down in my seat, wanting to melt away.

CHAPTER FOUR

Imogen, head downcast, returned to the table.

"Everything okay?" Jane asked.

"My friend I was meeting up with later cancelled."

By the slump of her shoulders, I guessed this friend was more than that, or Imogen wanted the person to be. Was that why Imogen had chosen the seat facing the front? Was this friend supposed to show up here?

"Why?" Jane pressed, one eye on me as she did her best to suppress her happiness over the news. I was gathering Jane didn't know about this so-called friend either joining us or stealing Imogen away.

"Her sister went into labor early." Imogen glanced around the room. Was she already concocting another reason to leave the table?

Maybe I should invent a dartboard with semi-plausible excuses? Make it a game of sorts for when Jane decided to play matchmaker. I imagined a play-by-play sportscaster saying in his golf whisper, "What's it going to be? My rabbit had babies, or a waterpipe in the apartment above mine burst, and I have to save my poor gran from drowning?"

"Is that all she is? A friend?" Jane asked.

I wanted to kick Jane under the table, but unlike the other dykes in my high school, I never took to soccer, which in hindsight was a huge drawback for moments like this one.

"Yes." Imogen tugged on the front of her shirt, drawing it away from her throat.

"Are you sure you don't want more—?"

"I'm not looking for complications." Imogen blurted, but she seemed to realize it might be best to soften her combativeness with the incorrigible matchmaking Jane. "The only relationship I'm contemplating at the moment is getting a dog."

"Is that right?" Jane straightened in her seat. "Rory was saying how much she missed her dog back home and was considering adopting one. Weren't you?"

I didn't have a dog. Never had a pet of any kind. I gulped some air and simply offered a half-hearted shrug, hoping that didn't equate to a complete lie. No matter what I said, I figured Jane would twist it to suit her purposes, and I wasn't comfortable with white lies, except from the ones that kept society functioning. Like answering no if a woman asks if she's put on weight. Nor was I the type to call someone a liar in front of witnesses or even in private, really. This coffee meetup was full of social land mines.

But Imogen turned to me, a stunning smile on her lips and her blue eyes glimmering with curiosity. She really was beautiful, and those big, honest eyes conveyed she didn't have a mean bone in her body.

"I do live across from a large park. I imagine it's paradise for residents and their furry children." *Furry children? Really, Rory?*

However, this only propelled her stunning smile to widen.

Unfortunately, Jane butted in. "Well, now you have a friend with a dog. It's almost like fate pulling you two together."

I threw Jane some serious shade.

Imogen laughed, the sound echoing pleasantly in my body. "Not sure you can toss in fate so soon since I don't have said dog yet. I'm contemplating. Nothing more. Nothing less."

"Details schmetails!" Jane waved her hand, implying *don't be ridiculous*.

Imogen finished her drink. "I best get going."

Jane's upper body rocketed to launch-ready status. "What? Why? You said your friend cancelled, so hang with us."

"I don't want to be a third wheel."

There was genuine panic in Jane's conniving green eyes. "Nonsense. The more the merrier." Then the panic morphed into desperation, and she reached for a phone in her bag, her eyes tripling in size. "Oh no! My flatmate…"

Was she pausing for dramatic effect or stalling to think of a plausible excuse? Imogen had already used the early-labor card, which I hadn't known was a go-to excuse. Of course, it could be true, but the timing was highly suspect.

Imogen seemed to be thinking the same thing given her narrowing eyes, but she attempted to come across as less confrontational.

I'd about reached my max for absurdity, and it was only ten in the morning.

"She's in hospital." Jane brought the phone closer to her eyes, as if unwilling to believe the words on the screen.

If I had more of a backbone, I would have demanded she hand it over so I could read the message, if there was one. As far as I knew, she was looking at the world clock function, trying to figure out the time difference with Hong Kong, a habit I still had, even though my plans to move there had been scrapped many months ago.

"Imogen, I hate to put you on the spot, but can you play tour guide for Rory today?" Jane fluttered her eyelashes, drawing attention to the mist forming in the corners of her eyes.

Thanks to Jane's time working with theater kids years ago, she still put on a good show.

"It's okay, Jane. I have plenty of boxes to unpack." I

picked at one of the flapjacks but didn't take a bite. Anything with oatmeal was on my *do not consume* list.

"You can't stay inside on such a beautiful Saturday. You're new here. These days are rare and are meant to be enjoyed. It's supposed to lash rain tomorrow. You can unpack then. You've wanted to visit the market since you were a kid, and now, you're sitting right around the corner. You can't go home." She said everything much too rapidly, not attempting to hide her desperation.

"I can wander by myself, though."

"You're terrible with directions, and it's your first outing!"

"It's not like I'm a child who's run away from home and is lost in a big city."

Imogen followed the action as if Jane and I were sparring tennis players.

"I can't leave you on your own, but I have to go to my friend. *She's in hospital*." Did her stressing the sentence mean she knew I didn't believe a word?

"It seems to be a trend today. And, I should add Imogen has never visited Portobello."

"Not on a market day, no," Imogen said and then added, "But I'm familiar with the area."

Jane leaped to her feet like Wonder Woman set to rescue a damsel in distress. "It's all worked out, then. Toodles." She waved and fled, her skirt flouncing around her.

CHAPTER FIVE

The café door shut, leaving us sitting side by side in complete silence. There was uncomfortable, and then there was whatever this was. Was there a word for five—no, one hundred times uncomfortable? My brain spun to find something to say to break the tension, but I was seething inside for being put in this spot in the first place. This wasn't how I pictured my time in London.

The words "I can't believe her!" flew from my mouth.

"Oh, I can." There was humor and understanding in Imogen's tone.

I turned my head to face the stunning blonde.

"I met her on my first day at uni, and she hasn't changed one bit. There's something to be said for that." Imogen tapped a finger on the edge of the table.

"That's true. It's one of the qualities I like about

her, even if she can be infuriating." I steadied my breathing. "Really, you don't have to babysit me. I've been to new places before." I tried to paste on a confident grin, but who was I kidding? Directions and I didn't mesh, although I had GPS on my phone, so I wasn't at risk of never finding my apartment. In all probability, it'd take a few attempts.

Worst-case scenario, I'd hop into a black cab. On my apartment shopping trip, I learned all the drivers had to pass a test, unlike American taxi drivers. Once when I hopped into a New York cab, the driver made me type the address into his phone, even though we were on the street I needed—it was pouring rain, and I didn't want to ruin my dress. Learning British cabbies knew the streets like the backs of their hands put me at ease. Even if my backup plan was silly since I was less than two miles away, and I had found my way here. The latter didn't always make much difference, I'd discovered.

Imogen studied me while those thoughts ran through my mind. Was she able to parse through my faux bravado?

Finally, she said, "My plans for the day did get cancelled."

I playfully crossed my arms and gave her my best detective stare. "How much of your story is true?"

"What story?"

"The whole friend's sister went into early labor?" I motioned for her to come out with it.

"Every single word." She slanted her head to stare into my eyes. "I promise." Imogen placed a hand on her heart, bringing my eyes to her tempting curves. "Let me see if I remember correctly. You want to explore Portobello Market because of *Bedknobs*—"

"And, *Notting Hill*. The movie."

"Naturally." Her smirk called my attention to her full lips.

"Does that mean you're a fan?" A bubble of excitement swirled inside me. Liking—no, loving the movie was one of the criteria to apply to be one of my friends. Not that there was an actual application, but I tended to keep score of good and bad ticks in columns.

"Can't say that I am."

The way her eyes dropped to her lap made me wonder. "Have you seen it?"

"No. But..." She reached for her phone from the tabletop and tapped the screen, giving me another chance to take in her features without being overly creepy. I could stare at her for hours but knew if I actually did that, it'd be wrongly construed. "Okay, we now have a guide for the walk."

"A guide? Did you hire someone?" I scrunched my forehead, my eyes bouncing around like I expected someone to magically appear.

She laughed. "Not exactly." Imogen set the phone down in front of me. "This site lists the places to see from *Notting Hill*. Should I see if there's something similar for *Bedknobs and Broomsticks*?"

"I'm not one for following directions," I confessed, feeling heat in my cheeks.

"Is that why Jane said I should babysit?" Her amused, but also kind, expression made me smile in return.

As I gathered my thoughts, which wasn't easy with those lovely eyes watching me, I said, "Let me see if I'm understanding this correctly. You said this area on Saturdays is for tourists, but you're willing to show me around?"

"If that's okay with you. I don't want to force you to spend the day with me." While it seemed like she tried to sound as if my answer wouldn't upset her, something in her eyes conveyed she wanted me to say yes.

My body was screaming, *Why are you questioning this?* My brain, though, was repeatedly pressing a bright red panic button. This wasn't the time to give in to the charms of a stunning woman with a seductive accent. No, this was the time to head home, unpack, and prepare for my first day in the office on Monday. While I was new to the London office, I wasn't new to the company, and I had my fair share of spreadsheets to sift through to hit the ground running. It was one of my traits and why I was able to work my way up the corporate ladder.

Instead, I replied, "Sure. Why not? I mean, Jane went to a lot of effort to make this happen. It'd be a shame to disappoint her."

Imogen nodded, relief swimming in her eyes. "Do you think she planned to ditch us the entire time?"

"Who knows? I bet she mentally did a happy dance when you announced the *baby on the way* news." I added, "You promise that wasn't scripted? All of this seems to be working out perfectly. Too perfectly. Did you study theater like Jane?"

"Tell you what. After spending some time with me, why don't we revisit this suspicion and see if we can get to the bottom of it? I can ask you the same thing. Did Jane put you up to this?"

I flinched, and my voice squeaked out, "Me?"

"This isn't Jane's first matchmaking attempt. Not with me, but she's done it for mutual friends."

"You can't possibly think I'm in on this. I mean, I've been acting like an utter buffoon. Look how I'm dressed compared to you, and my hair is probably a frizzy disaster since I don't have a hair dryer yet." It took about a nano second to comprehend all I'd blurted, and I burst into giggles.

Instead of running for the hills, she laughed with me, not at me.

Greatly relieved, I added, "She's told me she fancies herself as a matchmaker, but she's never shared her success rate." I rubbed my chin. "Does that mean she hasn't been successful? Jane isn't the quiet type."

A flicker of an emotion crossed Imogen's face, but I couldn't put my finger on what it conveyed. "So far, she's three for three for our mutual friends. I have no idea if she's done it for others."

"What does that mean exactly? They had one nice date? Or more?"

"All of them got together and are still to this day."

I whistled. "Does that change your mind about spending the day with me? You were pretty clear about not wanting female entanglements." That last word conjured some ways I'd like to become physically entangled, but I did my best to block them from my thoughts. Not successfully, I might add.

"No. It doesn't necessarily change my mind."

I chortled. "That didn't resound with confidence."

"I didn't mean it that way. No one is one hundred percent right. I don't want to be the one to break her streak, but… I was serious earlier. I'm not looking for complications."

"We're totally on the same page because neither am I. You're safe."

I swallowed, wondering why the flicker of disappointment across her face reverberated inside me.

CHAPTER SIX

WE STOOD OUTSIDE THE CORONET THEATRE, looking up. The whitish Italian Renaissance construction stood in stark contrast to the brilliant blue sky above.

I squinted. "I'm used to movie theaters being an ugly chunk of a building with zero personality in the middle of a soulless parking lot." My eyes panned the street, spying some shops and restaurants, none of them as spectacular. "Does it still show movies?"

Imogen consulted her phone. "This says it's more of a mix now. Poetry readings, live performances, music, and educational talks."

I nodded, taking in the details of the ornateness, still flabbergasted. AMC theaters could learn a thing or two. "I guess I'll have to add seeing something here to my London to-do list because it doesn't look open at the moment."

Imogen made her way to the entrance but then gave me a thumbs-down, the universal no-go sign.

I moved closer to her and said, "Do you think anyone would look at me funny if I wore goggles?"

She cocked her head to the side, as if I spoke in a foreign language. Finally, she asked, "Why in the world would you wear goggles?"

"Oh, right." I bonked my forehead. "You haven't seen the film."

"How do goggles factor into a rom-com? Does it take place underwater?" She looked even more confused, which was endearing, actually. People who pretended to know everything bugged the hell out of me.

I laughed. "I'd explain it, but I don't want to ruin it for you. It's quite funny, and you might actually watch the movie someday."

"That's a big might."

A cab driver laid on the horn, inching dangerously close to the bus in the turn lane, pulling my eyes away briefly. Did the cabbie expect the bus driver to gun it to get through the intersection? Imogen didn't react to the scene, making me wonder if it was a normal occurrence. I'd always guessed Brits were uber polite drivers, but apparently not.

"Are you against love *and* relationships? Is that why you don't think you'll ever watch the movie?" I returned my attention to the conversation thread.

Imogen held her palm upward, opening and closing

her fingers to form a ball. "How do you separate the two?"

"Easily. I've had plenty of relationships that were fun, but when I stepped back for a hard look, I figured out I wasn't in love with the person." Of course, that was mostly when I was in college. I hadn't had much luck with women as of late.

"What'd you do when you came to this realization?"

"I was honest with the person in question. I'm always honest. Well, at least ninety-five percent of the time."

"What about the other five percent?"

"Let's just say if my mom asks me if I think she's put on weight, I say no even if she has. I'm too young to die." I cracked a smile to show I was joking, about my mom killing me, not the lying about her weight.

Imogen started to speak but then closed her mouth.

"So, are you against love?" I asked again.

"You're forming a lot of opinions about me based on the fact I haven't seen one particular movie." She extended a slender finger in the air, her fingernail showing signs of a recent manicure.

I shrugged, not seeing why I shouldn't form an opinion. "It is the best rom-com in history, so it's weird you haven't seen it. Unnatural, even."

"Unnatural." She blew a raspberry. "Please. Next you'll be asking me if I don't believe in magic."

"I'm not following—"

"*Bedknobs*—"

I snapped my fingers. "Right, that should have been obvious, but I'm curious as to how you know the premise of the movie. Or, are you lying about not seeing it?" I added in a joking manner. "You're among friends. I won't judge you."

She seemed taken aback. "Why would I lie?"

"People do. All the time." I stepped out of the way of a family of five, the father pushing a stroller filled with shopping bags as if it were a battering ram.

"That's a dangerous blanket statement. Besides, you said you don't lie, unless speaking with your mum." Her expression conveyed many emotions, but her soft laughter implied she could understand on that level. "It shouldn't be hard to believe others don't as well. Shall we get going to the next stop on the tour?"

"Sure." The way she changed the subject from mothers seemed curious, or was it my honesty about lying in certain situations?

We moved to the pedestrian crossing, waiting for the light to change. Another red bus rumbled by, and my eyes followed it while I said, "You've stated you aren't looking for complications."

"Is that a question?" She briefly turned those lovely eyes on me. If only she knew the effect they had.

"It could go either way, I guess, but I'm wondering if it's really true."

"Yes."

"Because...?" I let the sentence hang while we made our way across the street, dodging people headed right for us and not giving way, something I became accustomed to in Boston, but the Coloradoan in me forced me to utter many apologies when making accidental contact.

"Complications are annoying."

I rolled my eyes. "Did someone stomp all over your heart?"

She turned to me with a slight smile. "Sounds painful."

"Does that mean you haven't experienced it?"

"I'm twenty-eight. Of course, I've had my heart broken. You?"

"Once. Last year."

This caught her interest. "Is that why you're focusing on your career and creating a must-do London list?"

I was fairly certain I hadn't said either of those things with her present, and I believe the accusatory lift of my eyebrows proclaimed that.

Looking bashful, she confessed, "I didn't mean to eavesdrop, but I did overhear some things. The café was pretty small."

I conceded the truth with a nod. "That could be the case. I hadn't ever put the two together, but it does make sense."

We walked past a pub with a bright yellow exterior, some people already inside. We veered to the left, the crowd getting thicker.

Imogen stopped in front of a bright blue two-story house and pointed to a plaque. "George Orwell lived here. He rented a room, and it was so cold he'd warm his hands over a candle flame before starting to write."

"We had to read *1984* in high school."

"Judging from your scrunched nose, you're not a fan."

"It was okay. Jane Austen is more my jam."

She nodded in a way that implied *of course* since my movie taste included *Notting Hill*.

We continued our walk, my eyes darting back and forth across the street, taking in the charming brightly-colored houses. "Okay, now that I've shared something about my heartbreak, it's your turn."

"Is this a quid pro quo?" she teased, stepping around an older woman walking her dog.

"If you want to label it, yes."

"Do you always dive headfirst into troubled waters?" She gave me side-eye.

"It's an American thing. Oversharing and looking for dirt."

"How do you know Brits don't?"

"Half of my company is made up of Brits. I've worked with enough to know they find my questions way too probing or outright rude. Am I being rude? I'm not trying to be." I stepped off the sidewalk into the gutter as the crowds were becoming more difficult to wade through, and I hadn't noticed any cars on the road.

"I haven't chucked you into the rude column." With a smile, she added, "Not yet."

I looked at her out of the corner of my eyes. "What column am I currently residing in?"

"How do you know I've already classified you?" She raised one eyebrow, which was sexy as hell, making parts of my body purr.

"A wild hunch, but I can see in your eyes I'm right. You're forming an opinion about me." With a finger, I drew a circle in the air.

"I wouldn't say opinion since I'm only starting to get to know you, but I find you intriguing, playful, and… I'm not sure what else."

"I'll take the first two." I stopped in my tracks. "Are we on Portobello Road?" I pointed to those words painted in white in the middle of the street.

"Oh, sorry. I thought you knew we were. George Orwell lived at twenty-two Portobello Road." She hooked her thumb back to the house as if that should have explained everything.

"Ah, I see. Are you an Orwell fan?"

"I'm a book person and enjoy seeing where they lived."

"And you haven't seen *Notting Hill*? Hugh Grant's character owns a bookshop." I jutted out a hip.

"I know. It's one of our stops. It's not on Portobello, but one of the side streets."

"Would you take a photo of me standing—?" I pointed to the painted words on the asphalt.

"As long as you promise not to get hit by a car, or Jane will never forgive me." She took my phone from me.

I looked right and left, not sure which way to expect traffic or if it was a one-way street. It was narrow, but I knew from my street that didn't mean it was one-way. There wasn't a car in sight, so I bounded out to stand for the photo, no doubt with a big touristy grin.

Imogen, to her credit, took the assignment seriously and got a few snaps from different angles.

Back on the sidewalk, she asked, "Where are you lumping me?"

It took me a second to recall the conversation about categories, and I shook a finger. "Not answering that one yet. You still haven't told me about your heartbreak."

"It was a lifetime ago."

"Being an accountant, I like numbers. Are we talking about a previous life or…?"

"You're an accountant?"

"Yes, but don't hold that against me." My eyes dropped to my flip-flops.

"As long as you don't hold it against me that I'm in insurance."

I laughed. "I don't know which is worse. Let's say our jobs are on equal footing of turning people off."

"On one hand, it's nice. When people find out what I do, they don't ask any questions. My sister is a writer, but most of the time she lies because she gets tired of people either saying, *Oh, I've always wanted to write a book*, or *Can you make a living from writing?*"

"The only thing I get is people joking for me to do their taxes even though I'm a corporate tax accountant," I said in a *most people don't understand what that means* tone.

"So, you look for ways for companies to save money?"

"That's part of it, yes. Don't you do that in the insurance biz?" I narrowed my eyes in what I hoped was a playful accusatory look.

"Yep. I'll never be known as a superhero."

"Unless you uncover a massive fraud in your company and blow the lid off it." I made a *kaboom* sound.

"Is that one of your goals in life?"

"To be a whistleblower? I haven't considered it, but if presented with the chance, I would like to think I'd have the courage to stand for what I believe is right." A scent tickled my senses and made me whip my head around, checking out the different temporary stalls. "Do you smell crepes?"

"Yes, right behind that crowd." She pointed to a crepe stand, where a man poured batter and then used a metal spatula to spread it onto the round griddle.

"Do you mind if we stop for one?"

"Not at all. You didn't seem to like the flapjack."

"It was not what I was expecting."

"Which was?"

"Pancakes." I added, "The American kind."

"Those are hard to come by here, but when I'm in the States, I love a good American diner. The way they keep filling up your coffee." She acted out pouring coffee into a mug. "I could sit in one all day."

"Are there any here? I know we're in Britain, but I've seen enough McDonald's to know certain aspects of Americana have invaded your shores."

"There might be one or two diners, and every once in a while, I do like a Big Mac," she whispered conspiratorially in my ear.

"Is that right? I'm liking this wild side of you."

"Liking a Big Mac counts as that?"

"No, but admitting it does." I waggled a finger. "By the end of the day, I plan to wiggle a few more deeply guarded secrets from you."

CHAPTER SEVEN

"Is that right?" There was a playful smile mixed with a sexy glimmer in her eyes, and I felt like she was issuing a challenge for me to do exactly what I said: get her to spill her guts.

"I have a way with people." I shrugged.

She didn't respond, but judging by her facial expression, I, indeed, was having an effect on her. And vice versa, since a flood of warmth zinged through my body, settling in spots that'd been dormant for weeks, if not months.

A family with twin boys, no older than two, toddling between their parents caught my attention. "Oh, look at them in their matching sailor outfits. How precious."

Imogen followed my gaze, her shoulders momentarily softening, but they quickly returned to rigid status.

"I can't tell if you think they're cute or are calculating the complications twins would add to one's life. Now that I know you're in insurance, I'm assuming you do a lot of calculations all day long." I pretended to punch numbers into a calculator. "Unless you're in sales."

"No, you're right. I'm involved in the numbers, and having one nephew about the same age as those two has taught me the ramifications are immense. Although"—she returned her gaze to mine—"some complexities in life are well worth it."

I folded my arms over my chest. "Wait. I need to process that."

"You can't read into everything I say to reveal some mystical piece of a puzzle."

"Why not?"

"There's no time at the moment." Imogen wore a gotcha grin and motioned it was my turn to order a crepe.

"Saved by a crepe!" I turned, but a thought struck, and I asked her over my shoulder, "Do you want one?"

She shook her head and took a step to the side.

Even though there were plenty of options for exotic or sickly sweet, I requested one with Nutella. No need to mess with a classic formula.

The man poured the batter and spread it out with his spatula while wiping his brow with the sleeve of his free arm.

I tugged my T-shirt from my front. "It's getting hot."

Imogen glanced up at the sky, shielding her eyes with her hand. "Getting close to eleven. It's only going to get hotter." She regarded the crepe maker and then said, "I'll be right back."

Confused, I simply responded with, "Okay."

The man added the Nutella, folded the crepe into a triangle, placed it in white paper, and handed it to me. I paid his coworker, a young woman who looked as miserable as the man. Were they father and daughter? I stood to the side, unable to pinpoint where Imogen had disappeared to.

She hadn't ditched me, had she? Was I getting too close to whatever secret she guarded with her life? The thought made me laugh, since so far, it was easy to talk to her after getting over the first twenty minutes of painful interactions. What did it mean that it took less than an hour to move past our first difference?

The crepe was much too hot to bite into right away, which was cruel since my stomach wanted it. If it was going to be difficult to find breakfasts I was partial to, I might have to start making pancakes or waffles at home before heading to work. At my last job, several mornings during the workweek, a handful of us would go to a diner for so-called planning meetings. It was the best part of my workday. While I loved numbers, their beautiful honesty, I wasn't particularly excited about my job. It was solely a way to support myself and the travel bug dying to be let loose in the world.

Imogen came out of a shop, holding a plastic bag aloft and grinning like a war hero returning home. She had this adorable, dorky side that quite simply endeared her to me.

"I got you something." She handed the bag to me.

"What do you mean you got me something?"

She looked down at the bag in my hand. "Exactly that. Open it and see."

Baffled, I peeked inside and saw a baseball hat. I handed the crepe to her and removed the hat from the bag. On the front were the words: *Age of Believing*. Under that read: *45 years of Bedknobs and Broomsticks*. "Oh my goodness. It even has the bed!"

"I did a quick search on my phone, and technically, it should say forty-nine years since it came out in 1971, but…" She shrugged.

"Who cares about that? It's probably been waiting in that shop for me for four years, like magic."

She wore an *oh please* smile, but I sensed she was forcing that expression when in reality she liked the idea behind my words.

I started to sing the Angela Lansbury song "The Age of Not Believing" from the scene when she preps the bed for their first magical flight.

Imogen smiled, and her cheeks reddened as she glanced around to see the reaction from passersby. One little girl with pigtails started singing along with me. Soon enough, a few others joined in. Even the crepe-maker smiled.

After finishing, everyone grinned, and one person tossed a coin into my hat. That propelled a few more kids to ask for money to give me. A little redheaded boy begged me to sing another song, and feeling guilty that kids were giving me money from their parents' wallets, I felt compelled to oblige. It didn't take me long to decide on the right one, and I started "Portobello Road."

The crowd around me grew larger, and this time, more people joined in, all of us singing and swaying in tune.

When we finished, people clapped, and I scored more coins in my hat.

The crowd dispersed, and I moved to the side to avoid any more requests.

"If you ever need a side gig, I suggest taking your act on the road." Imogen pointed to the coins in my hat.

"I fear my repertoire is quite limited and might only work in this setting." I waved to our surroundings. "I think I might have earned enough to buy you a beer, though. Not bad for two songs."

"I'm surprised you didn't make more. You have a lovely voice." She looked at me with awe.

My cheeks burned.

"I have to admit I wasn't expecting you to burst

into song when I gave you the hat." She shuffled on her feet.

"If you'd known, would you have still given it to me?" I gave her my best *confess all* stare.

She met my eyes, not intimidated in the least. "I'm only sorry I didn't earlier."

"What can I say? I love the movie and have seen it a gazillion times."

"Is that the technical term accountants use?" She waggled her eyebrows.

"It absolutely is." I took my crepe back and bit into it, Nutella oozing onto my fingers. After swallowing the bite, I licked my fingers, enjoying the fact Imogen watched me do so with evident delight. "Can you help me?"

She swallowed but nodded.

"This is messy. Can you put the coins in your pocket and put my hat on my head?"

"It would be my pleasure."

Was she hinting at something else with the way she said those words? I really hoped so, but it was best not to voice it. Let it be a secret between the two of us in the middle of the crowded market.

"You aren't the only one who's surprised, by the way." I took another bite.

"What do you mean?"

I forced down the food. "Thank you for the hat. That was very sweet, especially considering you're a hater of the movie."

"Hater!" she scoffed. "I haven't even seen it. Therefore, I can't hate it."

"Anyway, it was kind, and I'll always cherish it."

Her eyes landed on me again, and I loved the way she looked at me. "I'm glad, and I hope that's not the last time I get to hear you sing."

CHAPTER EIGHT

I stared into her eyes, the warming sensation I experienced earlier notching up a few levels. "I might be able to arrange that."

"I'm taking that as a promise, and I hate it when people break a promise."

I tapped the side of my head. "Making a mental note of that. What else do you hate?"

"I don't have a running list, but I'll let you know as we go."

"Please do. I'd hate to disappoint you."

"I doubt you could."

I groaned. "Statements like that set up any person to fail. No one is perfect. Expecting perfection begs to be let down."

Imogen crossed her arms and cocked her head to the left. "You really don't think anyone can be perfect?"

"No." I punctuated that with a rigorous head bob.

"I mean do you think...?" She swiped a hand over her face. "I wasn't saying someone can be perfect, but do you believe I'm the type expecting perfection?"

"You said I wouldn't be able to disappoint you."

"We may be discussing different things here. I don't expect or want perfection, but that doesn't mean someone will disappoint me by being themselves. So far, you seem to be very you." She spoke those words without condescension but appreciation, if not admiration.

"Huh." I chewed the inside of my cheek. "What makes you think that?"

"I pay attention to things."

"Is that a promise or a threat?"

Her soft laughter was alluring. "I've never considered it a threat, but I guess some would see it that way." She added, "Surely, not the likes of you, though."

I flicked a hand in the air. "There you go again. Putting pressure on me."

"Says the woman who gave a concert on Portobello Road. It seems you like some kinds of pressure."

Damn! Busted. "I only sang two songs. That doesn't qualify as a full-fledged concert." I hooked one arm through hers, pleasantly surprised she didn't flinch. "Come on. I have some shopping to do, and there's a stall right over there that's calling me."

We stood at a table set up on the street. "Look at

this antique silverware. My grandmother would love it. Can I put forks and knives in the mail?"

"No idea, but I can't see why not. I wouldn't advise taking them onto a plane, but the post—that should be different, shouldn't it?" Her forehead furrowed.

I checked the price and whistled, but they were for my grandmother, the one family member who was always in my corner. "I guess I'll find out."

While I went inside to pay, Imogen stayed put. At the register, I was able to watch the blonde pick up some items. An antique hand mirror. Teapot. Candlesticks. When she hoisted an old-fashioned hair dryer to eye level, her scrunched brow made me laugh. I was the type to buy an item like that for the pure whimsy of it, but she seemed mystified why someone was hawking a useless item. I'd bet money her flat sparkled with newish appliances and dishes, while I loved to trawl through consignment shops and Goodwill.

Paid up, I stepped out into the bright light, momentarily blinded. I yanked the bill of the hat lower.

Imogen reached for my arm, guiding me deeper into the market stalls, and it became more difficult not to bump into others.

Two down from the one where I'd made my first purchase, I picked up a butterfly pocket mirror. "My friend's daughter would love this." I held onto it.

After some more scrounging, I found something for my friend's other daughter and son.

"Do you always buy things for others and not yourself?"

I chuckled. "Yes and no. Every once in a while, when I find something I love, I snatch it up. But my new apartment is so small, and until I get everything unpacked, I don't know what I'll have space for."

"I'm not surprised."

"By?"

"Your tiny flat. Being in central London comes at a price." She squinted, and I wondered if she ever wore sunglasses. Not that I wanted her to hide those enticing eyes of hers.

"I imagine it does, but my company is footing the bill for two years, and the location sold me."

"What happens after two years?"

"My contract is up." I picked up a beaded bracelet but set it back down.

"Will you be out of a job?"

"No, but I may have to relocate. Right now, they're testing the waters here. The office in London is new. I'm the only one in accounting, but that won't last long since they're interviewing some locals to be in charge. They might expand or close up shop here and call me back to Boston. Or they might send me somewhere else in the world. With Brexit, they're not willing to fully commit yet."

"Oh." She turned around and stared at a bookstall across the street.

I followed her eyes. "That's right. You're a booklover."

She nodded. "Collector, actually."

"Let me pay up, and we can check out the scene."

She turned her head to mine, her stunning smile back in place. "I'd like that."

∽

AT THE TABLE, I picked up a red-bound illustrated copy of *Alice in Wonderland*. While the book wasn't a first edition, it was beautiful. Carefully, I thumbed through it and landed on the tea party illustration. "How lovely."

Imogen stood closer. "Is it illustrated by Charles van Sandwyk?"

I checked the front. "Yes. How'd you know?"

She hefted one shoulder. "Collector, remember?"

"Is this something you'd buy?" I snapped it shut and weighed it as if that factored into the calculation.

"I might, but my mission lately has been completing Churchill's Second World War series."

"How many are there?" I set the book back on the table and started scanning for Churchill's name.

"Six."

"How many do you have?"

"Five."

I gawked at her. "Are they out of print?"

"Well, no."

"Why don't you buy the one you're missing?"

"Because that takes the fun out of it." She gave me a saucy smile. "I like exploring used bookshops and markets, and the books must be first editions."

"Signed?"

"Not necessarily. But they should be in decent condition. I don't mind some wear and tear, because I think books should be read and loved."

"I'm assuming you won't buy from a dealer online."

She looked at me in all seriousness. "I would never do such a thing. Yes, I'd buy *The Girl on the Train* from them but not something for my collection. Half the fun is the hunt."

"Which book are you missing?"

"The third. *The Grand Alliance*." Her eyes swept the table, but I was pretty certain she already knew it wasn't there.

The seller, who'd been listening, made a disappointed sound.

Imogen quirked an eyebrow.

He said, "I sold the one you need last week."

"Here?" Imogen glanced around the market, seemingly with new appreciation.

"No. In my shop." He handed her a business card.

She studied it. "Ah, you're south of the river. I'll add your place to my rounds."

"I'd keep an eye out for the edition, but I wouldn't want to ruin your hunt." He grinned, bobbing his gray head in an appreciative way. Imogen was probably his favorite type of customer. A passionate one, whom I'd wager would part with a sum of money all for the sake of the hunt and completing a project.

Imogen thanked the man, and we moved on.

"Do you watch the show *Billions*?" I asked.

"No. Should I?"

"I like it. One of the characters has a prized signed collection of Churchill's set, but to raise cash, he has to part with them. His intention is to buy them back when he can. The hedge fund manager, who has a grudge with the man, buys the ones he sold, and then, to add insult to the injury, he gobbles up all available sets on the market."

Imogen whipped her head to me. "Who would do such a thing?"

"Someone with too much money and vindictiveness." I shrugged, knowing being a billionaire would never be in my future, nor did I have it in me to be so conniving.

"Is the Churchill fan the good guy?"

"Not really. They both have issues. It's hard to describe. It's a show about how people with too much power and money keep trying to destroy each other, wrecking their own lives in the process."

"Not sure it's my cup of tea." She pursed her lips.

"I can't see you liking it. Are you thirsty? I'm thirsty."

CHAPTER NINE

Imogen glanced around, landing on hanging flower baskets, which I was quickly learning meant the establishment was a pub. "It'll be packed, but if you want a half pint and to get out of the sun for a bit, let's hop in here."

"Visiting different pubs is definitely on my London to-do list." I made an exaggerated checkmark in the air.

"As it should be." Imogen opened the blue door and motioned for me to go ahead.

It was now a quarter to noon, but the place, as Imogen predicted, was crammed. In the corner, I spied a small table at the same time she did, and we both legged it to beat out a couple entering right on our heels.

Marking our territory by placing my bag on the chair, I pulled out my wallet. "What can I get you?"

"Let me come with you." She hung her rain jacket over the back of a chair.

We got into what resembled a line, and I craned my neck around some tourists in *Mind the Gap* T-shirts, chattering in German, to check out the options. "What do you recommend?"

Imogen, who had a few inches on me, scanned the taps. "I'm partial to Camden Town Brewery. Their Hells Lager is refreshing for weather like today."

"A glass of Hells on a hot day. Perfect." I bumped my elbow into her side, causing her to turn those amazing eyes onto me, making the beat in my heart speed up to *thump, thump, thump* per half-second.

She turned to check out the table situation, a few people hovering as if about to strike.

"Half pint of Hells?" I asked her.

She nodded.

"Go. I got this." I gently pushed her toward the table.

That made her chuckle.

After two more customers were dealt with, I ordered the half pints. The bartender nodded, not wasting time to speak, pouring the lagers and accepting payment with another nod. I left a pound coin, my last from my previous visit, on a beer mat, which finally pulled out a hasty thanks from the man before he hefted his bushy eyebrows to a guy behind me.

I took two green coasters from a rack and carried

the halves to the table, Imogen reaching for her glass to allow me to situate the coasters.

"Is Fuller's another brewery?" I asked after taking my seat, tapping the corner of the coaster.

"Yes, and they operate many pubs in Britain." She sipped her beer. "It's nearly impossible to escape their London Pride in pubs, especially in tourist areas. It's not as common as Guinness in Ireland, but it's a close second." She held two fingers a quarter of an inch apart.

I moved my head side to side to get a better read on her expression but gave up. "I can't tell if you're a fan or not."

"It's not my first choice, but my dad likes it. It might be safe to say it's the choice of old men. That or a bitter." She took a not so dainty drink.

"Bitter?" I tried to surreptitiously peel the back of my shirt off my skin, the heat taking a toll.

"It's a pale ale."

"So not a brewery but a type of beer. Like lager."

She nodded.

I sampled the Hells, pleasantly surprised by its crispness. "Score." I made a tick mark in the air.

She narrowed her eyes. "Who or what are you scoring?"

"Both you and the beer, of course."

"Well, thanks for letting me know." The way she spoke the words in her sexy tone had quite the effect on me, and I was sure I emitted *you're fucking hot* vibes. Her smile confirmed, I think, she was on to me.

I took another sip, wanting a distraction from the flood of confusing thoughts pinging through my head. "Are you close with your dad?"

There was a hint of understanding in her eyes, but she obliged my diversionary tactic. "I am, and my mum. My whole family, really. You?"

"I guess so, but I like to tease I'm the black sheep of the family."

"Because you're gay?"

"No, because I like math. They're all creative types." I waved a highfalutin hand in the air. "They don't understand why I have a *real* job."

"It's the same with mine." Her expression displayed shock, but it faded quickly. "Where are they?"

"Dad, a photographer, is in Colorado. Mom, a screenwriter, lives in LA. And, my brother is a singer, who technically doesn't have a home. He's the type who tweets he needs a couch to sleep on and gets fifty offers within five minutes."

"How does he vet them?"

"I haven't asked, and I'm not sure I want to know. The concept of couch surfing is a step too far for me, the wannabe world traveler. My terms involve a clean bed, private bathroom, and no strangers."

"None?" Her sly grin seemed to suggest that wasn't entirely true.

I swallowed and only managed to muster, "Um..."

As if wanting to give me a lifeline, she went back to the conversation at hand. "They pretty much cover the spectrum of the creative arts. Don't you classify yourself as a singer?"

"Not a professional one. Jake has a band and is building a following. They tour college towns, hence the not having a home base." I took out my phone and played a clip on YouTube.

"Not bad."

Setting my phone to the side, I said, "You mentioned your sister is a writer. What about your parents?"

"Mum paints, and Dad was a cartoonist. He's a pensioner now."

"Does that mean retired?"

"Yep." She knocked back some of her beer.

"You don't look old enough to have a dad who's retired."

She laughed. "There's a bit of an age gap between my parents. Mum is his second wife. My sister is much older, from his first marriage."

I bobbed my head, wanting to know more but unsure how to press on without being the stereotypical nosy American. Would I get past that worry? Imogen was becoming more pointed with her questions and comments as the day progressed, so maybe Americans didn't have the market on being confident.

She continued, "I'm having dinner with them

tonight. We meet every Saturday at my grandparents' local pub in Hampstead Heath."

"How very British."

She raised her glass. "Guilty as charged."

"Why does Hampstead Heath ring a bell?" I rapped my finger against one of my front teeth.

"It's a place for rambling, and the hilly heath is one of the highest points in London. Tourists love it."

I snapped my fingers. "That's right. Someone told me I need to check out the view."

"I do recommend it. And, Primrose Hill. Probably not during the summer or on a weekend, though."

I made note of both on my phone.

"You aren't kidding about having a must-do list."

"I moved to Boston after finishing college, and I always thought I'd have time to explore it. When I knew for sure I was moving here, I dashed around to mark some things off the top ten list, but I didn't make a dent. Now that I'm in London, I don't want to repeat the same mistake. I'm not getting any younger."

"You can't be older than twenty-five!"

"Twenty-seven."

She whistled. "In that case, maybe we should get you a cane. It's all downhill from here."

I bumped my knee into hers under the table. "Mockery? Really?"

"Another British trait."

"Tell me more about your British ways." The space

was tight, but I didn't think that was the only reason our knees still touched slightly.

"How much time do you have?"

"I have no plans in the foreseeable future."

"I have dinner—"

"With the fam." I cut her off, wishing there wasn't a ticking clock on our time together. "I am here for two years, though, so if you can't teach me how to be a proper Brit by this evening, maybe we can meet up again."

"Only if I fail?" She challenged with an arched eyebrow.

I leaned on my forearms, the table listing some. "Come now. There's no way you can give me a crash course in one measly afternoon."

"Are you sure you don't want to broaden your sample size?" She also leaned on her forearms.

Our faces were close together, and my pulse quickened. "Sometimes you have to go with your gut."

"Which is telling you?"

"To stick with the girl that brought you."

"I thought the phrase was *dance with the girl*." She tilted her head to the side, which I was learning she did when trying to figure out something.

"I prefer all-encompassing statements." I leaned forward a bit more.

She reciprocated. "About girls or in general?"

"I guess we'll have to find out."

CHAPTER TEN

"You know, the view from the top of St. Paul's is pretty spectacular as well." Imogen pointed at my phone. "You should add it to your list, and my company gives us two free tickets. As it happens, I haven't used mine yet."

"Two?" I asked in a tone I suspected came across as curiously hopeful.

She nodded, seeming to curb a smile.

"So, I could use one of them?"

"Who would you like to go with you, though?" She leaned farther over the table.

If we weren't in a crowded pub, I may have been brave enough to plant my lips on hers. "Let's see. Someone who's British." I raised a finger in the air and continued. "Stunning blue eyes. Sweet with a hint of sarcasm. Tall. Good with numbers. Terrible taste in movies. Do you know anyone by that description?"

She shook her head. "Sadly, I don't."

"Is that right? Because I think you do."

"Let me run through the options. Jane is terrible with numbers."

"I'm aware. She's not the one I have in mind." I pretended to toss her name out of the running.

"Who else do you know in London?"

"My landlord, who has a bad hip, so stairs are out."

She crinkled her nose. "Oh, there are five hundred and twenty-eight steps to the top and, of course, five hundred and twenty-eight down. I wouldn't recommend taking anyone with a dodgy hip."

"Well, that only leaves one other person in my limited circle." I pointed at her.

She placed a hand over her chest. "Me?"

"Why do you seem so surprised?"

"You said this person only has a hint of sarcasm. I'll have you know, as a Brit, it's way more than a hint. But, I understand why you said that. There's a wide chasm between Americans and irony." She held out her arms, moving her shirt in a pleasing way over her curves.

"Is that right?"

"It's a proven fact." She leaned on her elbows again.

"On what basis?"

"What?" She cupped an ear as some men in the pub screamed at a sporting event on one of the televisions.

"How did you quantify?"

"I quantify things all day. I'm actually a quant."

"With actuary tables, but I think you'll find not everything correlates with either-or suppositions." I pressed my arms together and joggled my shoulders, which may have inadvertently squeezed my girls together.

Her gaze dropped momentarily. "Fancy talk, that."

I heaved a dramatic sigh. "You can't say, without a doubt, Americans don't understand irony while all Brits do." I held up my hands, moving them apart and then back together again, as if I was playing the accordion. "Where's the gray area?"

"Don't believe in gray areas."

"I see. Is this a good time to say I swim in the gray areas?" I moved my arms like an Olympic swimmer.

"Why doesn't that surprise me?"

"Because I'm an earnest American who crafts to-do lists?"

Imogen pressed an index finger against the tip of her nose, grinning ear to ear. "I want to be clear you said it, not me."

"You know what?" I seized my phone. "I'm adding *Teach Brits Americans get irony.*"

Her eyes widened with feigned derision. "Every single Brit?"

"I only have one in mind."

"If it's the one I have in mind, I must warn you she's stubborn."

"I'm gathering that, but I'm persistent."

"I'm gathering that." She bumped two fists against each other. "Lots of friction between the two personalities."

"Yes, but you know, some friction can be a good thing."

"Oh, really." I definitely had her full attention. "Can you give me an example?"

"With an audience? I didn't see that twist coming." I winked at her.

Her cheeks reddened, but she didn't break eye contact. "I think you'll find I'm not all actuary tables."

I countered with enthusiasm, "I'm not always the wholesome American girl. Gray areas can be beautiful things."

She swallowed.

I crossed my legs.

A loud group burst through the door, pretty much snuffing out the vibe we had going, much to my annoyance.

"Shall we continue... the tour?" she said, seeming equally as annoyed by the disturbance.

CHAPTER ELEVEN

Outside of the pub, Imogen turned to me. "We have to step off Portobello for the next stop. Not too far, though. Will you be able to handle that?" She placed a supportive hand on my shoulder.

"I'll do my best to stay strong." I wanted to casually roll my neck to the side and place a kiss on her hand on my shoulder. Would that be overly weird or obvious? I determined yes to both.

She gave it a squeeze but let her hand fall. "You're so brave."

I gave her an exaggerated eye roll. "Lead the way."

We walked down one of the side streets, the crowd thinning, but still plenty of people in shorts and tank tops, showing varying shades of super pale to bright pink, no one having a deep tan. One older woman, in black nurse-type shoes, had an adorable corgi who didn't want to be outside on such a hot day, given the sluggish pace and grunting sounds.

Imogen met my gaze, clearly taken with the dog.

"Is that the kind you want?"

She shrugged. "I haven't looked into breeds. I think my goal will be to adopt. I'm rather fond of mutts."

"That surprises me given your book shopping needs."

"Books and dogs are in completely different categories. A book is a collector's item. A dog is a creature that deserves love, compassion, and a happy life." She smiled at me. "There's an organization that rescues dogs that would more than likely be put down. I'd like to save one."

The softness in her eyes spoke volumes.

"Here's the bookshop. It's not the one in the movie, but it's as close as we're going to get given the story in question is fictional. You know that, right?" she joked.

"I'm not that delusional. Or, is this you trying to show off that famous British snark?"

"Ouch." Her broad smile didn't convey she was upset in the least bit.

"Can you take my photo?" I handed off my phone, knowing she would.

I pointed at the sign, hamming it up with the cheesiest smile for my mom but also to see Imogen's reaction.

She snapped some photos, giving me a few directions, such as moving my hand to avoid blocking the sign.

After checking the photos, I said, "I'm sending this one to my mom. She loves the movie as much as I do, and she loves to tell people she worked on the script, even though she didn't." A few taps of the screen and it was off.

"Does it bother you she fibs about being part of the movie?"

"That's my mom in a nutshell."

"A liar?"

"Let's say she can embellish with the best of them." I slipped my phone back into my pocket. "Can we go in?"

"I was going to insist. I can't pass any bookshop without browsing."

"I'm logging that." I indicated tucking that piece of information into my memory bank.

"You do love to keep track of things."

"I absolutely do."

Inside, we browsed the fiction sections, and Imogen pulled *Girl, Woman, Other* off the shelf. "This won the Booker Prize, and it was shortlisted for the Orwell Prize. I've been meaning to pick up a copy."

I eyed the colorful cover. "You favor prize winning books?"

"Sometimes, but I also like to support female writers."

"Yet, you're on the hunt to complete your Winston Churchill set." I gave her a puzzled look.

"I'm many things, an enigma most of all."

"It's one of your most appealing qualities."

She turned to face me. "How so?"

"I like peeling away one layer only to discover something even more interesting." I acted out pulling back one layer and then another. "It goes back to the perfection conversation. I don't want that, but I like to see things that don't necessarily jive with my first impression."

"Which was?"

"Are you sure you want to know the answer to that?"

She folded her arms across her chest, the book pressed to her left breast. "I absolutely do. Even more now."

"Why?" I found it intriguing she used the exact same sentence I'd used only moments earlier. Was that her way of telling me she also kept track of things?

"Don't try to distract me. What'd you think?"

"Okay, but you asked, so no getting mad."

She nodded.

"I thought you were a little uptight. Not that I could blame you since I nearly dumped my coffee all over you."

She grinned. "I remember, but it seems so long ago."

"Your turn, what'd you think of me?"

She clutched the book tighter to her. "Promise not to hold it against me?"

I nodded, bracing on the inside.

"I thought you were flaky."

I let out a whoosh of relief. "I can be, especially before I have a cup of coffee."

"I never would have guessed you're an accountant."

"That's the best compliment I've had all day." I pressed my hands together, standing on my tippy-toes, but a pinkish cover caught my eye, snagging my attention. "Oh, I thought about buying this at the airport but didn't think I'd be able to settle my mind enough to read a book. Instead, I watched movies."

Imogen read the title, *"Where the Crawdads Sing."*

"It's in Reese Witherspoon's book club." My heart skipped a beat. "Did I lose points for admitting that?"

"Are we keeping points?"

"Accountant, remember. I keep track of almost everything. Even if I don't want to."

She took the book from my hand and read the back cover. "It sounds good. I'll get a copy."

"What if I give you my copy when I finish, and I can read the one you're getting? Or do you not share books?"

"I'm not as uptight as you think."

"I'm learning that." I made a *peeling back a layer* motion.

We stared at each other, my pulse racing.

Finally, she said, "Okay. But, I like deadlines."

"Of that I have no doubt. I'm a fast reader. Will a week give you enough time?"

She held the books, their spines touching. "Mine's bigger."

"Two weeks?"

"Nah, I can do one week. How do we do the handoff?"

"We could meet for dinner," I casually tossed out there, my eyes back on the bookshelves, trying to pretend I didn't ask her out on a book date. That was much different than a *date* date.

"Dinner?" She shifted on her feet.

"No commitment, of course. Aside, from handing off the book and eating a meal together. I know you hate complications." I leaned against a display table.

"Only ones that cause problems."

"Sharing a book doesn't fall into troublesome territory?"

"I do see one problem."

The air seeped out of my lungs. "Which is?"

"I like to discuss books, so we might have to set up two dinners. One to hand off the books and the other to chat about them."

"So, you're proposing two book dates?"

"Yes. Would that be acceptable?" It was her turn to squirm. "I know you aren't interested in dating while in London."

"I could get into book dates, though." My eyes scanned the shelves again with purpose: to find more titles to add for book chats, but I didn't want to seem overly eager and scare her off.

"Me too." Her blue eyes sought mine, pulling me into her orbit.

"Don't forget you promised to take me to St. Paul's."

"I haven't."

Had we finalized three dates in under an hour?

An older woman with a cane cleared her throat and waggled a hand as if saying she wanted to pass between us.

I stepped farther away, but kept my eyes glued to Imogen, who also didn't break contact.

CHAPTER TWELVE

IMOGEN SIGHED AND REACHED INTO HER pocket for her phone. After glancing at the screen, she said, "Can you hold this?"

I took the book from her, and she left the shop, phone pressed to her ear.

Doing my best to focus on browsing the shelves, I tried not to keep an eye on the woman pacing in front of the shop. When she raked a hand through her blonde hair, I felt guilty for witnessing it, even if I was fairly certain her goal wasn't to put on a show. Her shoulders stiffened, and her pacing became more goose-stepping. Was she trying to control her emotions or being told to toe the line?

The call continued, so I paid for both books and slipped them into my bag.

I had hoped by the time the transaction was finalized, Imogen would be off the phone, but that didn't happen.

I didn't know what to do: go outside and stand off to the side, or wait inside the shop to give her a semblance of privacy, which was that necessary given we were in public? However, when I made it to the exit, Imogen pocketed her phone.

I pushed the glass door open. "Everything okay?"

She raked her hair one last time. "Yeah, but I have to go to Hampstead earlier than I thought."

"Oh." I wanted to ask why, but she was clearly upset about something and not volunteering the information. Did she want me to press so she could vent, or did she want me to ignore her being upset?

Before I could decide on a course of action, she asked, "Are you hungry?"

Looking at my watch, I was surprised to see it was nearing one. "Lunchtime," I foolishly stated, still tongue-tied from not knowing how to handle the situation.

She nodded and surveyed the scene, which was more residential. "I know a Thai place near here. Do you like Thai food?"

"It's literally my favorite, but I should warn you I'm pretty boring and will order pad Thai."

Imogen smiled. "If that's what you like, you should get it and not feel like you have to apologize to me or anyone."

"Huh. I'm used to friends and family telling me I'm wasting a chance to live a little."

"Considering you up and moved from your birth country to Britain, I think the people who say those kinds of things should keep their thoughts to themselves." She tapped the screen on her phone and then waved for us to go right. "While we're heading back to Portobello, the final destination is not in the neighborhood at all. Is that okay? I can look for a different option."

"It's okay, really. I think an hour is my max of wandering through a crowded market in this heat. Besides, you mentioned Thai. I take lunch seriously. Absolutely no takebacks when it comes to food." I made a slicing motion with my hand.

"I wouldn't dream of it."

We fell into step again.

"Who tells you about wasting opportunities?" Her gaze was on her footsteps, but I sensed a brimming curiosity.

Somewhat taken aback she was fishing, I mumbled, "Uh—"

"I'm sorry," she rushed to say. "It's none of my business."

"No, no. It's fine. My family isn't shy about telling me how I should live my life. Like I said earlier, they're artistic types, and I'm a boring accountant. In their opinion, I should live on the edge in every other aspect of my life because the majority of my awake hours are filled with tedious spreadsheets."

"Family can be challenging." Her shoulders tightened up again, much like they had when she was on the phone.

"Is that who was on the phone?"

She nodded.

"Want to talk about it?" I tried to sound supportive, not dying to know what had upset her so much.

She glanced at me, and then her eyes turned to the white terraced houses, her lips locking shut.

"I feel like we're walking through a Jane Austen movie," I said in hopes she didn't feel pressured to open up to me. Also, it was really like walking through a film set.

That made her smile. "If you like this architecture, I recommend visiting Royal Crescent in Bath. It's an impressive example of Georgian architecture, and I think it's been used for some movies, including *Persuasion*. I'm not sure which others, though. There always seems to be another version of an Austen or Dickens adaptation."

"You seem to know a lot about history and places to visit."

"It helps on pub quiz nights." She laughed, her mood lightening with each step.

"Are you on a team?" We crossed Portobello and headed for a side street still leading in the direction of my apartment—I think. Some of the streets curved, and I kept losing track of north, south, east, and west.

"A few of us at work are regulars on Monday nights."

"Sounds fun."

"I'm rubbish when it comes to cricket and golf, but Matt rocks them." She motioned for us to turn right onto another residential street. "It's not too much farther."

"I really can't believe I'm walking in London. Everything seems so new and exciting. Not the neighborhoods, but the experience. On my way to coffee, I loved seeing the red busses and postboxes. I kept having to remind myself this is where I live. I really hope this feeling never goes away." I stepped to the side for an older man with a dog to pass.

"Let me show you something." She led us to a red postbox on a corner. "When the worker empties it, he or she changes the tab marking the day. This still says Friday, meaning today's batch hasn't been picked up yet."

"Is it weird that I love learning this? Something similar probably happens with boxes in the US, but I never noticed because why would I? It's not foreign. I don't want to get to the point where I take things for granted. I feel like I've been given a new lease on life, and I don't want to blow it."

She gazed at me, and I wondered if I'd been too

earnest in saying all that. But she said, "You know what you should add to your list?"

I had to stifle a *you get me smile* to simply say, "What?"

"There's a wait list for it. Maybe three or four months, but you can sign up to witness the locking of the Tower of London gates. It's called the Ceremony of the Keys, a seven-hundred-year tradition, and no one is allowed to take photographs. I haven't done it myself, but I keep meaning to. It's an ancient military ritual, and it's my understanding it's only been delayed once over seven centuries."

"What happened?" We crossed a quiet street and turned onto another, making me question how I'd find my way back to my apartment.

"There was a bombing raid in World War II."

"That's understandable, then."

"Still, the man in charge felt so bad he wrote an apology to the king."

"Can you imagine missing something at work and having to write the king?" I chewed on my bottom lip.

"It does put some things in perspective, yes."

"I hate when I have to send an email to my boss if I'm running a few minutes late because the subway is having problems. A regular occurrence in Boston."

"Transport in London also has issues, but the TFL app is useful. It helps with arrival times for trains and busses. If you do ride a double-decker bus, promise me you'll go to the top and do your best to get a seat in the front."

"Adding a mental note to download the app, and I absolutely promise about the bus. Who wouldn't want to ride on the second level?"

It was her turn to flash her *you get me* grin.

I wanted to circle back to the family comment, but I still didn't feel I knew her well enough to push. However, it seemed like we were quickly becoming old friends. To a point.

CHAPTER THIRTEEN

"Here we are." Imogen waved to a brick pub, the outside of it nearly covered with flowering plants.

I could barely make out the name of the place, the plants taking over everything, including the sign of... I squinted, covering my eyes to read *Churchill Arms*. "It's like the pub is a living, breathing organism." I continued gawking, seeing some windows, but again, the plants were the star attraction. "I wonder what Churchill would think. If I remember from my history classes, he was a larger-than-life character. Would he like the flowers stealing the limelight?"

An odd smile appeared on Imogen's face. "Let's see what you think when we go inside." She opened the red door and waved me in. "After you."

Walking inside, my eyes took a few blinks to adjust from the blinding sunlight to the darkness of the pub.

Every seat at the bar was taken, as well as the tables. Many stood wherever there was room, huddling close.

But that wasn't what Imogen had meant, because as my eyes grew accustomed to the dark, I started to take in all the Churchill memorabilia on the walls. It was as if a museum curator was determined to display every newspaper clipping, photo, and advert so no square inch of wall was visible.

I looked over my shoulder at Imogen. "I stand corrected. Churchill would indeed love this place."

She grinned and crooked a finger. "Follow me."

Imogen led us past the bar and a fireplace that I imagined was a delightful place to sit with a beer and book on a cold winter day. She kept going, the pub giving way to a restaurant. Once again, plants hung from the ceilings, green vines dangling down like we'd transitioned to a jungle.

"This place is a trip." I continued to eye the ceiling, my mouth slightly open.

"It's not the typical English pub, but I've always liked it. I'm pretty sure Winston would have gotten a kick out of it."

Unlike the pub portion, the restaurant wasn't nearly as packed, and a woman led us to a table for two, leaving us with menus.

After she left, I laughed. "I'm sorry. I'm still in shock about this place. When I got out of bed this morning, I was beyond cranky, and I had no idea my day would turn out this way. It's been such a delight."

"Why were you cranky?"

"A beeping truck, followed by my landlord yelling at the driver, woke me minutes before my alarm. I hate waking before my alarm. Like I'm being robbed of sleep."

"Duly noted," she said, a blush creeping up from her neck, and she quickly added, "Would you like a beer?"

"Sure. Do we order them here or at the bar?"

"Here, but I should have warned you they only accept cash in the restaurant part."

It was my turn to blush. "Uh, I only have the coins that I believe are still in your pocket, which I was supposed to use to buy you a beer with, but I forgot you had them. I have no idea how much my singing netted, but it's probably not enough for lunch. I spent my remaining change from my apartment shopping trip earlier today, and I haven't stopped at an ATM yet. On Monday, I have to open a checking account here." I closed my menu, feeling silly for giving such a long and convoluted excuse when all I needed to say was I didn't have cash.

"Tell you what. I'll get this since it was my idea. I didn't even think that you wouldn't have your accounts set up." She bonked her forehead.

"All part of the joy of moving to a different country. Although, I had the same problem when I moved from Colorado to Boston. I had an account at the Bank of the West, and I felt like an idiot when I asked a teller if they had any branches in Beantown. Before then, I never considered I'd limited myself by my choice. When I was in college, I had no idea where life would take me. I guess I still don't." Again, I'd blabbered, but Imogen gave me all of her attention, making me feel like she enjoyed learning these tidbits about me. She didn't go into long explanations herself. I didn't hold it against her, even if I wanted to peel back more layers.

I scanned the menu, quickly locating the pad Thai options at the top. "Are prawns like shrimp?"

"I believe so." She peered over her menu.

"What's your go-to here?"

"I'm always partial to Panang curry in any Thai place."

I read the description: spicy red curry with coconut milk, basil leaves, Thai lime leaves, and peppers. "Sounds good."

The waitress returned to take our orders. Imogen selected prawns with her curry, and I opted for chicken with my pad Thai.

"Are you ever tempted to read your Churchill books here? I noticed the fireplace. That'd make a great reading spot."

"They have another fireplace on the other side, but the one we passed is my favorite. I should warn you it's hard to get the chair near it. Some of the people here are regulars, and I hate taking a seat when an older person wants to sit. I end up standing at the bar most times or sitting in here."

"One of my exes was the type who never gave up her seat on the subway. It simply didn't cross her mind if she saw an elderly person, a pregnant woman, or a parent cradling a baby. It drove me batty that I'd have to tell her to get up."

"I never sit on the Tube."

"Why is it called that?" I leaned back for the waitress to set down our pints.

"It's officially called the London Underground, but it got the nickname because some of the tunnels are round tubes. Also, half of it runs aboveground. That's always made me chuckle."

She seemed much more relaxed since the phone call, and maybe it was the heat mixed with a few sips of beer, but I opted to go full-American. "Why did your phone call upset you so much?"

"It didn't, really. Rather, that's how I am whenever I deal with family." She rested her elbows on the table. "Since my sister has a young son and I'm not attached, it's expected that I do the majority of babysitting, even though my sister only lives a block away from my mum and our dad. I know she has her hands full with work and Charlie, but I work, and it takes me an hour to get to their place. Dad is in the beginning stage of dementia, and my mum is in denial. My sister's mum wants nothing to do with him, and I can't blame her. Dad tossed her aside for my mum and started a new family. Our brother wants nothing to do with any of us."

Apparently, I'd been wrong. Imogen was capable of information dumps if I asked the right question. "You have a brother?"

"Greg. He's fifteen years older than I am, so I never got to know him. We have the same father, and that's the extant of our closeness."

"So, he doesn't go to Saturday family dinners?"

She let air seep out of her puffed cheeks. "He's a man, so it's not expected."

I didn't want to tell her this, but I loved complicated family dynamics because mine was a quagmire. "If I remember correctly, your sister is much older, but she has a toddler?"

"Yep. It's her second marriage, and I think Charlie was a surprise. She got up the duff in her mid-forties."

"Up the duff. That's a new one." I laughed. "No wonder you don't want complications."

She half-smiled. "I haven't even filled you in about our cousins."

"It gets more complicated?" Mentally, I was rubbing my palms together in a *bring it* fashion.

She nodded, but her willingness to share the dirt seemed to come to a close.

"Wow," I said, my mouth forming an O.

If her cousins were even more of a shitshow than her immediate family, I couldn't blame her for not wanting to add another human to her dynamic, the realization settling uneasily in my stomach. I guess it served me right for wanting to hear that it wasn't only me with a crazy family in this world.

Back in college, I used to wish I had normal parents like many of my roommates and friends, but now, I accepted I wouldn't have the American family seen in cheesy Hallmark Christmas movies. For the most part, it was easy to forget them, aside from holidays and birthdays—okay, I guess it wasn't all that simple to blot them from my thoughts, and it required a lot of mental gymnastics and pretending I, without a doubt, loved it being just me in this world.

CHAPTER FOURTEEN

"Would you excuse me for a moment?" I got up and made my way to the bathroom.

I looked back over my shoulder to see Imogen checking her phone. Was there another message from a family member?

The passageway to the bathroom was lined on both sides by overgrown plants, some of the vines tickling my legs as I swept by. When I opened the door, my arm brushed under the hand dryer, causing it to roar to life, and I stifled a scream because my brain first thought a tiger had leaped out at me.

With a hand over my racing heart, I gathered my thoughts. Imogen had stated that she didn't desire any snags in her life, and honestly, did I want to venture into treacherous family dynamics during my stay? It was easy to see in the tightening of the crinkles around her eyes that they drove her insane. I had my own family to drive me bonkers. No need to add a different branch to the crazy tree.

However, it'd be nice to have someone who understood cray cray family, whom I could confide in, not solely my friends with their perfect relatives. They tried to understand, but it was like explaining space travel to Jane Austen. Or so I imagined.

And, had she said she spent every Saturday night with them? That was a prime date night. Or it was for me. Did she see them every Saturday even when she was dating someone?

After washing my hands, I fixed some random strands of hair, and exited the restroom to see Imogen on the phone again.

All the signs were pointing to keeping her in the book club category. Nothing more and nothing less.

I retook my seat, displaying an *I'm sorry* expression for interrupting. She rolled her eyes, making me smile.

"Okay, okay. I'll leave right after lunch." She circled a finger around her temple.

I forced a smile, but my insides went cold.

She set down her phone. "Sorry about that."

"I get it." My expression hopefully conveyed my second language was lunatic.

There was silence. I hated silence normally, and this one really made me uncomfortable. So, I launched into a story. "Back in Boston, I lived in an apartment complex, and those of us in the back had decks. The lady who had the deck next to me, but one floor up, was one of those crazy people it was best to avoid eye contact with. It was difficult when I went out onto my deck because she was always outside doing some type of home project. Painting a door or something like that.

"I prefer being outside for three seasons out of four, so I decided to build a plant wall, but when I moved to Boston, I was fresh out of college and broke. On my walks through the neighborhood or around my office, I would collect plants people set out with the trash and nurse them back to life. Once I walked into my office with a half-dead tree, and after I whizzed by with my head down, my boss said, *Did Rory walk by with a tree twice her size, or am I having a seizure or something?*" I laughed over the memory, but at the time, I'd been mortified.

Imogen offered her killer smile, and I crossed my legs.

"Over the months, my wall became quite impressive." Once again, I eyed all the green in the restaurant. "Not to this level, but it did the trick. After a couple of years, I'd blocked my neighbor out completely." I leaned on the table. "Here's the kicker, though. When it came time to pack up for the move, none of my friends wanted any plants. Not one. I didn't have the heart to throw them out after I'd saved them. My annoying neighbor and I had one thing in common. The love of plants, so I gave them to her."

"Wait." Imogen lifted a palm in the air. "The

woman who inspired the plant wall got them in the end?"

I nodded, snorting with laughter. "Life is funny."

She laughed with me. "It really is."

"I'll miss them. The plants, I mean. Not her."

"Do you get them back when you return?"

"Oh, I doubt it. She asked for my email to keep in touch. I think she's hoping to stay with me for a cheap trip to London, but that's not going to happen." I made a *no way Jose* gesture.

"Why? Besides not liking her?"

"I gave her a fake email address."

Imogen grinned, twisting a purple stud earring. "Is that something you do often?"

I wanted to know why she was asking, but the waitress arrived with our meals, and I lost my nerve. Probably for the best, given the whole family situation, her desire for no complications, and my two London goals, which weren't coming to my mind at the moment, but I knew they were important this morning and would come back to me. Everything was stacking in the cons column, and I should simply accept that.

Her phone buzzed again, and she read the message on the screen.

I really shouldn't press her on it. Not at all. But, my heart asked, "Your sister?"

"Mum."

"Oh, the one-two punch." I pretended I was a boxer mimicking those actions.

"Something like that."

"Why are they so worried?"

Her eyes dropped to the table. "I'd texted saying I couldn't make it tonight. Apparently, that's not allowed."

"Not allowed?" I shouldn't have said that with such disbelief, but how could a woman in her late twenties not be able to stand up to her family? I had to caution myself that not everyone had a family like mine. We loved each other (at least I told myself that), and part of the reason for that was we hardly ever spent time together. The Price family was firmly in the *absence makes the heart grow fonder* category (again something I said to myself when spending another occasion alone). "Has no one ever missed Saturday night dinner other than your brother?"

"Yes, of course. But not me."

"There's a first for everything."

"Yes," she said in a tone that implied, "But, not today."

We tucked into our meals, an uncomfortable silence pressing down, and the plants hanging over our heads made me feel even more stifled. Was it a British-American thing? Were they more family-centric? In college, my friends were amazed when I proposed ski trips over Christmas break, since most of them went home for the holidays. Out of the past eleven Christmases, I'd only spent one with my mom and another with my dad. The time with my mom, I was a junior in high school and was scouting some colleges in California. The one with my dad was during my last year at home.

Imogen's mood plummeted to an uncomfortable level, so I did what I do best. Perk someone up with a funny family story. "When I told my dad I was moving to London, he asked me if it was safe to drink the water here?"

"Where does he think London is?" She scrunched her brow.

"Oh, he knows I'm in Britain. He's a strange man. When I was younger, he wasn't so bad. But the older he gets, the more unhinged he becomes. He's turned into a conspiracy nut and sends me articles and books about crazy shit. I chuck whatever he sends without looking and never click on any links he shares in emails. If he does visit me here, I bet he'll only drink bottled water, no matter what I say."

"I always pour bottled water into a glass. There's something about drinking from the plastic container that puts me off." She shrugged as if saying she hadn't reached my dad's level of paranoia. "Your parents are divorced, right?"

"Yeah. My mom loves to tell me divorcing my dad was always her plan. Her parents were the super religious and strict types, so she saw marrying my dad as her escape. Originally, she only wanted to stay with him for a few years, while she built a nest egg, and then bail to California where she lives now.

Having my brother and me delayed her plan by five years."

Imogen's jaw dropped.

"I know. They really are odd people. I love them, but I don't want to spend a lot of time with them, and having an ocean separating us is a major plus." I tossed in, "I'm pretty sure the feeling is mutual."

"At the moment, I'd like some space from mine." She seemed uncomfortable admitting that and changed the conversation. "Do you have a lot of unpacking to do?"

I'd shared more than I normally did about my parents, so I appreciated her diversion. "Mostly personal items. My apartment is furnished. It's kinda weird for me to sit on a couch that others have, but it does make things that much easier. It even has a TV, and my internet and cable were hooked up before my plane landed."

"You can watch telly tonight, then."

"I'll probably read. For our book club. Oh, don't forget yours." I opened my bag and set hers on the table. "I'd hate to steal it from you."

"I didn't even know you'd purchased it. Thank you. I guess that means we're squared."

I twirled noodles onto my fork. "What do you mean?"

"For the meal. You don't owe me any money."

"But—no. They're not the same thing." I held my fork halfway between my plate and mouth, a peanut plopping onto the food. "I'd like to take you out for lunch or dinner to pay you back."

"It's not necessary, though."

My heart plummeted to the pit of my stomach, initiating a roiling sensation. Why did that bother me so much when the items in the con column were screaming to be shoved to the side? "I don't always ascribe to necessary and unnecessary. It's the Bohemian quality in me."

Her lips thinned.

Whoops, my American snark landed like the Hindenburg at a birthday party.

Should I apologize? Pivot? Scarf my meal and make a clean break for it?

"Will you be taking the Tube to work?"

I wanted to laugh, but I also felt relieved that Imogen was doing her best to change the subject yet again. "Yes. I'm pretty sure it's a straight shot from Lancaster Gate to St. Paul's, if my relo person can be believed."

"Relo?"

"Oh, sorry. It's stands for relocation. The company has been moving a handful of us over, and we have a Slack channel to help us navigate all the hoops. It's made me feel less lonely." I swallowed a mouthful of beer, wishing I hadn't used that word. I tried never to say or feel it.

"I think you're very brave to uproot from your country." She ran a finger down the side of her glass.

"I have to remind myself I'm not here on vacation. On Monday morning, I have to get on the Tube and head to the office. I might do a dry run tomorrow, as silly as it sounds."

"I don't think it's silly. Ye Olde Watling is a nice pub near St. Paul's. Or, if you feel adventuresome, there's The Blackfriar, located next to the river, probably a five-minute walk from the station. It's built on the location of a Dominican friary, and inside, there are stunning reliefs, mosaics, and sculptures of friars." Her eyes grew larger with excitement. "Nearly every pub has their own character and history. Like this one, which I love because of the Churchill angle, but almost every pub has its own twist. I've been working on a book, a mix between tour guide and history book. It's how I spend my Sundays. I pick a spot on the map and go for a wander to find pubs."

"You don't do any preparation before your walkabouts?"

"I like the element of surprise."

"That," I stopped myself from saying *surprises me* and switched gears to, "sounds fun. I may have to steal that idea." Maybe she was more amenable to my Bohemian personality than I initially thought.

"It's the best way to get to know a place. Start walking and see what you find. I see so many tourists with their noses stuck in guidebooks, and they forget to look around for all the little details, not the ones listed in the top-ten things."

"Have you secretly been mocking my to-do lists?" I leaned forward, grinning.

"Not at all. Like today, you didn't really have a plan for Portobello, aside from going. I was the one who looked up sites to see, but early on, I got the feeling you'd rather go at your own pace. I admire that."

"I completely forgot about the guide we were *following*." I made quote marks. "But, I'm glad we came here. This is a place to remember if any of my family visits." I stifled the urge to add, "God help me."

"Have they mentioned they will?"

"Threatened is more like it. My dad and brother more than my mom." I ran a hand through my hair. "If they make good on the threat, more than likely, I'll get a call after one of them lands here, and they'll want to meet up for drinks, possibly dinner."

"Would your brother sleep on your couch?"

I shook my head. "I sincerely doubt that. He'd probably do his Twitter plea for a place to stay."

"I… I don't know what to say about that."

"I always thought it was because they're creative types, but so is your family, and your nearly on the opposite side of the spectrum. Maybe my family doesn't like each other and has accepted it without verbalizing anything, and I've been blissfully turning a blind eye." I hefted a *what can you do?* shoulder, knowing I wasn't being completely forthcoming. How does one say to a woman they find interesting: *I can't stand my family, but don't hold that against me?* Especially to a woman who spent every Saturday with hers?

"Sounds lonely."

"No, it's not." As I said the words, a nagging thought worried at the back of my brain. What was my reason for all the back-and-forth thoughts about my family? Not just today, but all the time. I thought I knew how I felt about them, but did I really? Did I simply not want to admit to myself or anyone I was indeed lonely? Not that Imogen's situation seemed ideal. There had to be some type of middle ground.

CHAPTER FIFTEEN

"I'm sorry. I didn't mean to imply anything." She looked like she'd stepped on a puppy's tail.

"No, no. It's not that. I don't mind when people make observations or challenge my belief system. I actually like that." I set down my fork. "I've never ever thought about this or tried to put it into words. When I signed up to move here, many of my friends asked if I'd be okay being so far from my family. I thought even asking such a question was completely preposterous. Like they were the ones with the issues and wondering if they would pass up an opportunity of a lifetime to stay close to home." I placed a hand on my chest. "Am I the one with the issue?"

Imogen didn't move a muscle.

"I'm not asking you to confirm or deny. Is my family dynamic wrong or hurtful even? I won't deny there's comfort having the Atlantic as a barrier, and in my mom's case, there's the ocean and then the entire continent separating us since she's on the west coast. I never have to consider her when I go about my normal everyday life, because in all probability, she won't come here to visit. She thought Boston was a backwater and nagged me to move to New York City. But I didn't have a job in the Big Apple. London is probably a step above for her, but her making the effort—that's not in her genetic makeup." Apparently, not in mine, either. I took a long pull of beer. "She liked calling me her half daughter, because after my parents divorced, I was only with her for school holidays and part of the summer. Even then, I spent more time with a nanny than I did with her." I eyed Imogen, the family person, to gauge her reaction to everything. "I'm judging by your squirming that I'm on to something. Should I add therapy to my London to-do list like one of my friends suggested?" Whoopsie! That was probably one step too far, and I tried laughing it away, but it was a pathetic attempt.

Not seeming put off, Imogen leaned over the table, as if wanting to confide only in me. "I think you're asking the wrong person, because I don't know how to stop my family from making demands of me. Like tonight. My sister wants to have a drink with her husband before dinner to discuss something, and she wants me to watch my nephew. She sprung it on me, and when I said I was busy, she spat out trawling through used bookshops didn't take precedence over my nephew. The thought I might be with another human being didn't even cross her mind."

"Do they know you're gay?"

"Yep and they were fine with it before I accepted it. I think it's a relief to my sister, on one hand, because she doesn't view any of my relationships on equal footing as hers since she and her husband have a child. They're a more cohesive unit that's been part of family structures for centuries." She threaded her fingers together. "Man, woman, child. I'm an outlier, so clearly I can live by different rules, meaning if I have a partner, said partner shouldn't ever feel slighted if my sister wants to go to the pub with her husband, forcing me to dash over to watch my nephew." She shifted in her seat.

The waitress buzzed by, but our body language must have made her realize now wasn't the time to ask us if we needed anything because she didn't stop.

Imogen continued, "I adore my nephew and love spending time with him, and if my sister gave me advance notice, it wouldn't rankle. But she doesn't even think to give me notice, because I'm Immie, viewed as the spinster aunt of Victorian novels, and I should appreciate any crumbs they send my way. I wish there was an ocean and continent separating me, but saying that makes me feel guilty. Why should I have to go so far away to live a normal life without their expectations butting in?" She sighed. "I'm sorry.

I've never told anyone this." Imogen tugged on her collar.

"I like the nickname," I said, wanting to reach for her hand but not knowing if it'd be welcomed, especially in a public space.

"My friends and family call me that."

"Can I?" I held my breath.

"I think my meltdown qualifies you as a friend."

"If that's your idea of a meltdown, I'm cringing about when you see me really lose it. Two words: not pretty."

She gazed into my eyes. "That's hard to believe, but I've learned people handle emotions in a million different ways. There's not a right or wrong way. Only your way."

"Are you always this logical?"

"Unfortunately." She let air slowly seep out of her lungs, looking defeated.

"I don't think that's bad."

"Others have."

I blew a raspberry. "You know what? I'm tired of those people. The ones who are always telling others how to be, the way they should live their lives, what's appropriate and what's not. It's fucking exhausting to please everyone else and not take into consideration that doing so makes me miserable. This is my first day in London, but I'm calling it now. It's my first day of my new life. A bolder, happier, more confident Rory Price. Look out, London—no, world."

CHAPTER SIXTEEN

Imogen laughed, siphoning off some of the tension from her shoulders. "The entire world is on notice."

I stretched my arms overhead, my neck releasing a satisfied pop. "I'm feeling nice and light. More importantly, in the moment." I wagged a finger at her. "You should tell your sister you can't babysit. We can get ice cream and stroll through Kensington Gardens. I want to check out the Peter Pan statue. I've always liked the idea of the story."

"The child who refuses to grow up." Her expression was the perfect mix of intrigue and ridicule.

"Yeah. I'm aware I have a grown-up job, but I don't want to be a *grown-up* grown-up, you know? If I want to take off on a Friday night and head to Paris, I'm free and clear to do that."

Imogen knocked back some of her beer. "That does sound nice."

"Should we go?" My spine shot to ramrod straight.

"To Paris or Kensington Gardens?" she joked, clearly not taking me seriously.

I tried not to let her lackadaisical attitude infect me, because I thought it was a brilliant plan. "Why not both? I'm serious. I don't have to be at my desk until nine in the morning on Monday. Isn't the train ride only a couple of hours? We could leave tonight and come back late on Sunday." I wiggled in my seat, growing more and more excited by the prospect. Maybe Jane was right. I should expand my to-do list to include Europe, not solely the United Kingdom.

Imogen looked down at her plate, her fork stirring the food, but she didn't prepare a bite. Nor did she speak.

Shoving aside the crushing feeling, I said, "It's a fun thought," to let her off the hook.

"Would you excuse me for a moment?" Imogen headed for the restroom.

The remaining fumes of exhilaration whooshed through me as the realization settled inside. Not everyone would pick up and do something crazy simply because I wanted to. Also, Imogen barely knew me. This wasn't like that Ethan Hawke movie where two strangers get off a train to spend a night together exploring Vienna.

If I was on the train and met a fascinating woman,

like Imogen, would I have gotten off in a city I didn't know, with a person I'd met that very day? Deep down, I knew I would have. Because when my company asked for volunteers to uproot their lives, my hand couldn't shoot in the air fast enough. I craved new and exhilarating experiences. My eyes fell to the remnants of my pad Thai. Well, not always, but did my boring food choices define me completely? Not at all.

Did I need someone in my life who had the same itches that needed scratching?

That was more difficult to answer, given my recent revelations about my family. The day had taught me I did want someone in my life. Jane was spot-on about that. But, I needed someone who got me.

Could a wild child and a family-oriented person meet in the middle?

As I ran through a hundred and one relationship scenarios, Imogen returned, looking even more downcast.

"I'm afraid I have to go."

"Was it the Paris thing? Can we forget I said it?"

"No, it wasn't Paris." She smiled, but there was something behind it that didn't sit right. Was she lying to me? To herself? "My sister is insisting I need to come early to watch my nephew. She says it's urgent. More than likely it isn't, but she's a writer and…" Imogen let out an angry sigh. "I'm really sorry."

I wanted to argue that going to the pub with her husband wasn't a dire need, but what was the point?

Imogen had already flagged down the waitress for the bill, and it wasn't like I was qualified to handle family situations. Both of us, apparently, had issues when it came to that.

After paying the bill, she said, "Do you know how to find your way home?"

I shook my phone side to side. "This will guide the way. I still might go in search of Peter Pan before heading back to do some unpacking."

"It's on the palace side of Long Water."

"Okay, thanks." I had no idea what Long Water was, but I didn't want to press, either. The last message or call from her sister must have been a doozy.

We walked back out into the sunshine, my bag over my shoulder, Imogen clutching the paperback.

"It was lovely meeting you." I wanted to give her a hug, but an invisible wall had been put up.

"It was." She shifted her weight, looking as if she couldn't wait to make a break to be with her family, the lesser evil at the moment.

"Don't forget to read the book, or our discussion won't be nearly as fascinating." *That is if there isn't another nephew emergency.*

She tapped it against her thigh. "I won't let you down. I better get going."

"Safe travels." I wanted to take back those words, because it sounded more like a goodbye instead of a *see ya later*.

Her face twisted up into confusion, but she simply nodded and turned around to leave.

I walked in the opposite direction, not knowing where I was going but needing some space. It wasn't until I reached a busier street that I realized we hadn't exchanged numbers.

Was that a sign? That neither of us thought to ask?

Not wanting to dwell, I activated my maps app to figure out where in the heck I was. I was on Kensington High Street, and if I went left, I'd make it to the gardens, where I wanted to explore. Imogen said the statue was on the palace side of Long Water, which I was assuming was an actual body of water. I extended the map and was relieved to see Peter Pan was on it. I marked it as my destination, and the voice told me to continue along the street I was on.

There was a crush of people on the sidewalk, many women carrying shopping bags, and I felt like a salmon fighting upstream. Unlike when I walked in Boston, I couldn't help but stop and take things in. Even little things like TJ Maxx being called TK Maxx here seemed overly charming.

I remembered I needed a hair dryer, so I hopped inside. Unfortunately, I didn't find what I needed, but I purchased a bathrobe since the large windows, which provided natural light, didn't offer much privacy.

While in line, I googled *why is T.J. Maxx called T.K. Maxx in England*. As it turned out, when the American retailer wanted to expand, there was already a discount store called TJ Hughes. I preferred to think T.K. was T.J.'s younger brother who wanted to break out on his own.

I really did have family issues.

After I paid, I made my way back to the street, and soon enough, I reached an entrance of the gardens. Heading down the path, the palace came into view, and I stopped in my tracks. This was something you didn't see in the United States. Following one of the paths, grass on both sides of me, I noticed little kids having soccer practice on my left and a man chucking a tennis ball for his dog on my right. This park was a part of their everyday lives, and in front of me was the palace where William and Kate lived with their family. How fucking weird.

I shook my head but couldn't get over the fact that this was now a part of my life. In the mornings, I could put on my running gear and exercise here. With a palace right there.

Rory, you're not in Kansas anymore.

CHAPTER SEVENTEEN

I stood outside the entrance of the palace, looking at the Queen Victoria statue, the white marble standing out against the dark blue sky, the afternoon heat pressing down on me. A terrier mix trotted nearby, proudly carrying a tennis ball in his mouth, causing him to make snorting sounds.

To the side of the palace was a carousel, and the happy sounds of kids laughing and screaming in delight filled my ears.

In front of the palace was a pond, where children fed ducks, geese, and swans, the latter of the group acting pretty aggressively. After consulting the app, I was certain this wasn't the water I wanted. Giving the scene in front of the palace a final sweep, bringing a smile to my face, I moved to one of the paths cutting through the grass, which seemed like it headed toward the water.

Even though the sun blared overhead, there wasn't much humidity, a blessing after living in Massachusetts for a handful of years. Again, I was taken by how many people used the park for their summer weekend entertainment. There was a group playing volleyball, loads of picnickers, and it looked like there was a trapeze school, if the sign could be believed. Wouldn't that be a kick?

Would Imogen even contemplate signing up?

I shook off the thought. This wasn't about her. It was about me exploring my new city, much like a child whose dream had come true.

I spread out my arms, twirled, and said, "Dude, I live in London!"

A few heads turned, but most people kept to themselves. That was in tune with city life on the East Coast. Crazies were normal, diluting their abnormal behavior. It got to the point that I noticed when people were polite instead of shoving their way past me. A sad state but an accurate one for metropolitan life.

My eyes swept my surroundings, spotting a large golden object to my right. According to my map, it was the Prince Albert statue, but I didn't veer from my course. Today's mission was Peter Pan. Maybe each day I should have a different goal for my runs. Keep it stimulating, because while I usually ran four times a week, I wasn't the type who loved it. I did it to stay in shape, and I hated gyms. The stench, creepy guys, and way too many mirrors—no, thank you.

Water came into view, and I consulted the map again. It looked like once I reached it, I needed to hang a left. I wished everything about my life was this simple. So far today, I'd made my way to the café on my own, and now I was strolling through a fancy park with a palace on the horizon.

The path leading to the statue had a railing on my right, lots of trees and bushes behind the fence. Little birds hopped on the branches, occasionally taking flight, before landing farther away from me.

I stopped to watch a squirrel, who slipped through the railings, inching closer and closer to me, clearly used to tourists feeding him.

"I'm sorry, Earl. I don't have anything to offer you."

My newly named friend—naming things was something I did—sat on his haunches, doing his best to look even cuter to get me to give him something.

A large dog dashed by, and Earl scrambled up a tree.

I continued along the route, skirting past a man and woman, their arms around each other's waists, walking at a glacial pace, not noticing anything surrounding them.

And then there it was.

Or I guessed it was there based on a tour group, the adults snapping photos on their phones, while the kids chased each other on the surrounding grass, screaming. Not one of them checked out the statue. While I waited for the tour group to move along, I stood by the railing, watching the ducks and some other birds I didn't know floating on the water.

A grey heron perched on a piece of wood sticking out of the water. Then my eyes spied a bird fitting for the regalness of the park. He had an orange crest of feathers on his head, like royalty. I gave George—that was the only kingly name I could recall on the spot—a little wave. Then, I spied a black swan skimming the surface of the water, off on his own, unlike the two white swans across the way making a heart with their necks.

I watched the black swan with curiosity, unable to banish the thought that his solitary existence was my future. Heck, it was my present as well. Would others always see me as an exotic creature but not as a mate? Not for life?

Again, I thought back to the Paris conversation with Imogen. Was it simply my fanciful talk that had scared her off, or was there something else?

My phone vibrated, and I answered after one ring.

"Is your roommate okay?" I asked Jane.

"Wh—Yeah, she's fine. What are you doing?"

"I'm waiting for a crowd to leave so I can check out the Peter Pan statue."

"The what?"

"A statue in Kensington Gardens." I moved to the side so two people could get a photo of the heart swans, neither of them paying attention to the black swan I named Colonel Brandon, an underappreciated character in *Sense and Sensibility*.

"Oh. Are you with Imogen?" Jane's voice brought me out of my head.

"No, she had a family thing." I tapped a finger onto one of the points of the fence railing.

"What'd you think?"

"About what?"

"About Imogen."

"She seems… nice." I tried to sound lighthearted.

"You can't admit it, can you?" She sounded smug.

"What?"

"You two are perfect for each other."

I laughed, kicking a stone off the path. "I really think you missed the boat on this one."

"What happened?"

"Nothing. She's nice. We wandered Portobello for a bit, chatted, and then said goodbye."

"No plans to meet up?"

There was no way I was going to tell her about our book club, which I was certain was dead in the water. Again, my eyes sought out Colonel Brandon, remembering Alan Rickman carrying—who played Marianne Dashwood in Ang Lee's production? I saw the movie five times in the theater. Her name was on the tip of my tongue. *Come on, Rory.* The chick in *Titanic*, but I constantly confused her with Cate Blanchet.

Jane rudely cut into my daydreaming. "I'm coming

your way for dinner. I need a full debriefing to see where you went wrong."

"Where I went wrong?" My voice cracked.

"You two are meant to be together. I've never felt so right about something in my life. I'll meet you at your flat around seven. We'll go someplace near you."

I started to protest but gave up after figuring out she'd hung up.

Jane might think I was meant to be with Imogen, but Immie didn't think that. The crowd dispersed, and I was able to get a photo of Peter Pan without another soul in the shot, not even me. Before leaving, I took a snap of Colonel Brandon and whispered, "I appreciate you."

CHAPTER EIGHTEEN

AFTER I PUT THE BED UP AND TUCKED THE remaining boxes into a corner behind one of the wingback chairs, there was a knock on the door.

"Coming." I gave my studio one final glance, knowing it was the best it was going to look given I'd only had a couple of hours to unpack some things before Jane's arrival. The biggest accomplishment was sorting and putting away all my clothes in the walk-in closet, which was one of the nicest features of the place.

I swung the door open.

Jane had her arms crossed and was tapping a foot. "Why are you so stubborn?"

I rested my head against the door. "Why do you always think you're right?"

"Because I am. The sooner you accept that, the easier it'll be."

"You know that's probably why you play matchmaker and why you don't date much. Relationships are about compromise—meeting in the middle." I looked her up and down, her combative stance not giving in. "You want to come in?"

She walked past me into the main area. "This is much better than what I was picturing." Jane spun in a circle in the middle of the room, which gave her the whole experience really. "It's been freshly painted, and the arrangement makes it seem so much bigger."

"My landlord is an interior designer." A gay one, so that explained the closet.

"Is that the bed?" She pointed to the large closet-like doors.

"Yep. Would you like a drink here, or do you want to head out? I managed to hit a couple of stores on Queensway but haven't done a proper shop, so the choices are severely limited."

"Let's find a place where we can sit outside."

"Perfect. I was thinking we'd go to the Italian place on my street. My dogs are barking after walking in flip-flops all day."

"So California of you."

I grabbed my bag, and we headed out.

A bespectacled man with a deep five o'clock shadow led us to a small table, right next to the dry cleaner. The owner of the shop, whom my landlord had introduced to me the previous day, stood out front, smoking a cigarette and staring at his phone.

When he noticed me, he smiled warmly, flicking ash onto the sidewalk.

This didn't escape Jane's notice. "Already making friends, I see."

"It's something Americans do. Smile and say hi. You should give it a go."

"Is he American?"

"French, I think."

"Be careful. While you're being friendly, he may have other things in mind."

I laughed. "He's in his sixties and gay."

"How do you know he's gay?" She leaned closer, wanting the dirt.

"He used to date my landlord."

"Your landlord is gay?"

"Yeah. I think it gave me an edge when I was apartment shopping."

"Huh. You've only arrived in this country, and you have two more gay male friends than I do."

I didn't believe this for one second, but there was no use challenging Jane on some things.

A waiter arrived to take our drink order, and we opted to split a bottle of Gavi, a white wine from Piedmont, Italy. He'd promised it was the perfect fit for the balmy night.

I let the previous conversation fade, not wanting to rile Jane, who had passionate thoughts on most subjects. It was one of the things I liked about her. All the late-night conversations at camp, about anything and everything under the sun. After camp, we stayed in touch, and we would meet up once a year in New York to catch a Broadway show. Her passion for theater never dwindled, and she occasionally picked up bit roles for local productions. She was one of my friends from my college days that I'd stayed in contact with, which given my conversation with Imogen earlier, I wasn't the type to stay in touch with many, not even my family.

The waiter poured two glasses of wine after letting me sample it. Then he took our food order. We opted for two antipasti choices: prosciutto and melon and insalata caprese, consisting of tomato and buffalo mozzarella. Jane selected spaghetti al pesto Genovese, which had garlic and pine nuts, and I opted for something more sinful: penne alla gorgonzola. I was a sucker for anything with blue cheese and had never paired it with pasta before. I continued to tick off firsts in life.

"How long until this sinks in?" I took a sip of my wine, my eyes watching the happenings on my street. I waved to the pub across from us, groups of people congregating outside, drinking beer, talking, and laughing. At the other end of the street was another pub, two news shops, and a small grocery store, which I'd learned earlier had exorbitant prices and not many options.

Her eyes followed mine, looking bored. "It's London. No big deal."

I smiled at her. "Says the woman who goes gaga over Burger King in the US."

"I don't know why you moved from America. The Burger Kings aren't the same here." She jutted out her lower lip.

I laughed, knowing she was completely serious about the topic. When I'd told her I accepted the job in London, her first words were literally, "But, Burger King."

Jane folded her hands on the table. "Tell me where you went wrong today."

"Nothing went off the rails today. I had coffee with you, until you skipped out on a fake emergency." Jane didn't attempt to correct that statement, making it clear that was indeed what had happened. "Imogen and I did some exploring together. We had lunch. I walked through Kensington Gardens. I made friends with Earl the Squirrel—"

"Earl the Squirrel," she said in her over-the-top mocking tone.

I was glad she'd butted in before I blabbed about Colonel Brandon, knowing she'd use my fanciful daydreams against me and say I was losing my mind due to loneliness. It wasn't like I was the only woman who wanted to be rescued in a rainstorm, and I wasn't bi, but Alan Rickman was kinda hot in that role.

I said, "It suited him. Much more so than Duke the Squirrel or Baron. I have to admit I know nothing about British nobility." I tried to sound serious, like

THE SETUP

that was the only disappointment from the day. Not Imogen rushing off after I mentioned going away together to Paris.

"Why are you having dinner with me and not Imogen?"

"You asked."

Jane narrowed her eyes. "Confess."

I set down my glass. "Why do you think I'm at fault?"

"What aren't you getting? You and Imogen belong together." She traced a circle in the air with her index finger.

"If that's the case, we'll have to wait to see what happens, but it's not looking good. I don't even have her phone number."

She whipped out her phone. "Ready?"

"That doesn't seem right. If she wanted me to have her number, wouldn't she have given it to me?"

"She can be a bit peculiar about certain things."

"Like her family."

Jane looked upward as if searching for something in the heavens. "She lets them walk all over her."

"I picked up on that." During the antipasti course, I filled Jane in on bits and pieces of my conversations with Imogen.

When our pasta meals arrived, Jane's expression had darkened some, but she still said, "I know I'm right. We'll have to figure out a way to nudge Imogen to take a chance."

"Am I that scary?" I covered my heart. "I think I'm very low on the intimidation scale."

"Oh, please."

I slanted my head. "You think I'm intimidating."

"You're beautiful. Confident. Adventurous. You know what you want and won't settle. That can be off-putting."

"All this time, you've been saying we're a perfect fit. Your words. Not mine." I jabbed my fork in her direction.

"You are. The yin and yang."

"I've never understood what that means."

"It doesn't matter the actual meaning. When you slot your personalities together, you two make sense." She laced her fingers.

I stabbed two penne pieces with my fork. "Thinking something should be true, doesn't make it actually happen. Besides, my original problem still exists. My time in London has a ticking clock. This"—I motioned to the street again—"and that"—I pointed to the greenness of Kensington Gardens behind the wall —"are my focus while I'm here. I want to soak everything in before I go home."

"Where's home for you?"

"Boston. That's where my company is headquartered, although there's talk about them opening up an office in San Francisco, so fingers crossed." I did so with my left hand, while placing the pasta into my mouth with the other. Swallowing, I said, "Oh my God, this is delish." I gobbled two more pieces.

Jane wouldn't let herself get sidetracked. "If you keep moving, you'll never settle down. And, San Francisco is in California, much too close to your mum."

"First: didn't you list adventurous as one of my qualities?" I forked in another bite. "Second: San Fran is in Northern California and is three hundred and eighty-one miles from LA." Maybe it was bad I found this place so soon, but I was envisioning many evenings here, gorging on blue cheese pasta; never mind the weight I'd put on.

"How do you know the mileage?"

"It was the first thing I did when I heard about the office. To make sure there was enough of a buffer."

"Okay, let's go back to the travel part. Wouldn't you like to explore the world with someone by your side?"

"I imagine flying with a dog isn't easy, and good luck getting a cat to behave."

Jane leaned back in her seat, crossed her arms, and stared me down. "You can lie to yourself all you want, but I'm not buying this *I only need me* act."

"It's not an act or a lie." I avoided her eyes.

Jane swooped up her phone from the table. "If Imogen texted me for your number, you wouldn't care if I shared it?"

I was certain she was bluffing, because the timing

was too perfect. "Share it or don't. I'm not going to get my panties in a bunch."

Jane set down the phone, not touching the screen.

I smiled smugly, but inside, my bravado sunk like a stone.

CHAPTER NINETEEN

We ordered dessert, tiramisu to share, and our waiter gave us free shots of limoncello.

"What's your plan for the rest of the night?" Jane asked, sipping her shot.

"Shower and bed." I forked in a bite with the right ratio of Mascarpone cheese filling, espresso-soaked ladyfingers, and whipped cream, letting out a delighted moan.

"Living on the edge."

"I did arrive yesterday and haven't had a moment to rest. I'm not a college kid anymore." I set down my fork. "Were you wanting to hang or something?"

"Nah. I have plans in Soho later."

I checked the time on my phone. "It's a quarter to nine."

"The day is only getting started." She waggled her brows.

"You kids today." I yawned into my hand. "I'm fading fast."

"Poor you." Jane softened her expression.

The check arrived, and I tossed down my credit card. "This is on me."

"Why?" Jane jacked her eyebrows to her widow's peak.

"I do appreciate your matchmaking effort, even if it failed. Aside from the ending, I had a nice day. Thank you." I squeezed her hand.

"If only all my clients paid me for my services." She winked.

"Do your other clients know ahead of time, or do you spring it on them like me?"

"There's something about the spontaneity of meeting someone."

"I'm not sure it counts as spontaneous if you plan it." Also, I learned the hard way Imogen wasn't the spur-of-the-moment type.

"Oh, come on. You had no idea this morning in the café that you were sitting next to your soul mate until I introduced the two of you."

"Soul mate!" I squealed. "If that's truly the case, I better adopt a dog, because that's the only way I won't end up alone."

"So, you are worried about being alone." She wore a gotcha expression.

"Nope. Nice try. It was simply a joke. A bad one at that."

The waiter took my card and inserted it into a handheld machine. He seemed pained that a piece of paper came out that required my signature, reminding me I needed to set up a bank account so I could use a pin as my coworkers who'd already hopped the pond advised. The man returned with a pen, and I scrawled my name on the line.

We had to go back inside to leave via the door because I didn't trust my ability to step over the red rope delineating their patio dining from the sidewalk.

I gave Jane a hug goodbye.

"You sure you can find your way home?" she joked since I was less than twenty feet from my front door.

"It's going to be difficult, but I'll fumble my way there."

"Be careful who you fumble with. No picking up strangers now that you and Imogen are an item." She threaded two fingers.

"You don't quit, do you?" I gave her my *let it go* glare. "Go to Soho. Have fun, but be safe." I waggled a mom-like finger.

"I never behave. Not sure why I'd start tonight." She waved, walked toward the end of the street, and turned left for the Tube entrance.

I opened the gate to my stairs, wincing when the hinges protested with a hideous sound. I glanced up, expecting to see Nigel hanging his head out the window to chastise me. Nothing happened, and I left the gate open, feeling fairly secure with the crowd outside the pub. Tomorrow I'd find WD-40 or the British equivalent.

Inside my apartment, my brain started to concoct to-do lists for Sunday. Get groceries, not merely the basics in my fridge. Finish unpacking. Set out my work outfit—oh, I needed an iron to press my trousers and blouse.

Sighing, I closed the curtains, blocking out the world or at least the lower-half of people walking past my window. Stripping out of my second outfit for the day, I hopped into the shower.

Unfortunately, the water had the opposite effect on me, and when I finished, I was wide awake. I opened the curtains again, but I had zero desire to sit inside all alone. Not on such a beautiful night. I didn't want any more booze, so I grabbed a water bottle from the fridge. My relo person had supplied the basics, such as a small carton of milk, half a dozen eggs, bread, and cheese.

With wet hair, and only wearing a tank top and basketball shorts from my college days, I climbed my steps and sat on the top one to soak in the atmosphere. I brought my new book in case the mood to read hit me.

Across the way, a middle-aged man in a New York Yankees T-shirt stumbled on his feet, sloshing his beer over his shoes, regaling his group with something that he thought hilarious, but it seemed like his travel buddies had reached their fill. Were they family? Old frat buddies? One of the guys put his arm over the drunk's shoulders in an effort to get him to head to the hotel next door. There were at least five on this street alone.

But the man refused to budge, saying, "One more."

His friends let out a collective sigh. Had this been the experience the whole trip? Was I staring at my future? Traveling with single friends, either being the obnoxious drunk or having to put up with one?

At one of the tables, a man and woman sat with their teenaged son and daughter—or so I assumed since the kids were the spitting image of the father—enjoying the evening, the teenage son holding court, his parents laughing, while his younger sister exhibited the perfect eye roll only a teen could do.

I drank some cold water, the still air becoming more pronounced.

Two guys in cutoff jeans and no shirts, walked by, each holding onto a handle of a beer cooler. Both were bright red. Had they been drinking in the park all day without sunscreen? I didn't envy their showers tomorrow. Even with cold water, it was going to smart.

I cracked open the book, literally. I never enjoyed reading a paperback until I broke the spine, not once, but three times.

"I see you abuse books."

I whipped my head around to Imogen.

"What are you doing here?"

"I was in the neighborhood." She cradled a potted fern.

"Not buying that story."

She smiled. "I wanted to drop this off to welcome you to London."

"You're swinging by to give me a housewarming gift?"

"I was going to leave it outside your door. Jane said you were knackered. You don't look it. Did you lie to escape Jane?" She wore a *you can confide in me* grin.

"My shower gave me a second wind." That was when realization sunk in, and my hand went to the back of my head. "I must look a fright."

"Not at all." From the way she nervously shuffled on her feet and cradled the plant against her, another realization swept over me.

"Would you like to come inside?"

CHAPTER TWENTY

"On second thought, I don't have anything to offer you, unless you want bottled water." I rushed to add, "In a glass. I do have some."

"Water would be great." Her face was red, and the shade continued to deepen.

"Did you have to walk far?"

"No, but the train was boiling, and it really hasn't cooled off much this evening." She plucked her shirt away from her skin.

"Cold water might help." I started to descend the metal stairs, and Imogen followed me.

With my hand on the door, which was slightly ajar, I said, "Don't judge the *just moved in* state of my apartment."

"I wouldn't dream of judging you about anything." Her eyes drilled the truth of her words into me.

"I actually believe you."

"Do you not normally?" The corners of her mouth twisted upward.

"I'm not the most trusting of others, so no."

Her thoughtful nod suggested she understood, or possibly she was on the same page.

We entered the main room. "Welcome to my pad."

She scanned the room. "I was expecting so much worse. Where are all the boxes?"

I pointed behind one of the chairs. "Jane came over before dinner, so I did some rearranging after a quick shop for some necessary items."

Imogen gave an appraising look. "I wouldn't have even guessed you recently moved in."

"I didn't bring a lot of my stuff."

She cocked her head. "Does that make you sad? I know you miss your plants, but do you miss other things from back home?"

I squeezed the paperback close to my chest with both arms. "Not really. I was a kid when my parents divorced, and watching them squabble over things but not really putting up much of a fight for who got us"—I tapped the side of my head—"that left an impression. I think a part of me vowed from a young age not to get bogged down by objects that didn't have meaning in my life. I'm more about living life. Being free. Traveling. My friends became my family. The closest I ever came to getting a pet was my plant wall. Oh!" I relieved Imogen of the plant.

"Wait. Didn't Jane say you missed your dog back home?"

"Busted!" I chewed on the inside of my cheek, holding the plant close to me in both arms. "Does it count as lying if I didn't correct Jane because I worried she would twist whatever I said to her benefit somehow?"

"I think I can let it slide given the circumstances."

"This little guy is going to love the window." I set him on the sill.

"It's a Boston Fern. I thought you might like a piece of your plant wall back. Not literally but symbolically."

"That's really sweet of you."

She stared at her shoes.

"You're going to love it here, Roscoe." I checked the soil, which was damp.

"Roscoe?" Imogen laughed.

"I name everything, and he looks like he has wild hair. Very fitting for a Roscoe."

Instead of looking bewildered, she simply said, "Of course, you do."

"Is that not a thing here?"

"Quirkiness?" She boosted an eyebrow.

"If you want to slap a label on me, yes." I jutted out one hip.

"I've never named a houseplant, but I'm only one person on the island, so it's hard for me to generalize if that's a British trait or not." Her teasing smile did wonders to appease the loneliness I had been feeling since we parted after lunch.

"Point taken! You never back down. I like that." Would I think the same if I saw her around her family? "Now, make yourself comfortable, and I'll get you the water I promised."

In the kitchen, I grabbed the last bottled water from the door of the fridge and pulled down a glass, noticing for the first time, none of my glasses or mugs matched. I opened one of the drawers, and the silverware was a mismatched disaster. That brought a huge smile to my lips. I poured her water into the glass and went back into the room.

Imogen sat on the love seat, not one of the chairs flanking the room. That had to be a good sign, right? Unless she expected me to sit in one of the chairs. Or, was this a test?

"Nothing in the kitchen matches," I crowed.

She took the glass from me after I sat down next to her. "What do you mean?"

"The glasses, mugs, silverware—none of it goes together." I laughed. "I absolutely love that."

She chuckled with me. "You really are like no one I've met."

My laughter stilled, and I studied her face. "Jane swears you're my soul mate."

"She mentioned that to me via text."

I knitted my brow. "She's positive about it. At

dinner, she accused me of messing up. Do you think she's on to something?"

"That you messed up?" The corners of her eyes crinkled.

"Oh, nicely played." I slapped her thigh ever so slightly. "I meant the soul mate part."

"I figured. I'd be hard-pressed to give a true definition of the word."

"Oh." I sipped water from my bottle, unable to figure out what that meant. Did she not believe the concept existed? Or think two people were never quite compatible for the long haul? It was best to enjoy the ride while it lasted?

"But, that doesn't matter much to me. Defining things. Or assigning labels. I know you accused me of putting a label on you, but I really don't. Me clarifying something isn't labeling."

"What is it?"

She started to speak but then raised a finger. "You set a trap!"

I circled a finger in front of my face. "Woman."

Imogen feigned being shocked, but her eyes sparkled with humor.

"How'd it go with your family? Did your sister have a true emergency?" I asked as a way to give her some space, while my brain whirred about the whole soul mate concept. Also, I'd be lying if I said I wasn't curious about her evening considering how much her mom and sister annoyed her all day.

"No emergency and the evening was fine." She looked away.

"I'm going to let the topic go for the moment, but if you plan on visiting Roscoe in the future, he's going to need more information about your family and how you fit into it." Where in the fuck did that come from? I wasn't the type to put demands on someone I barely knew.

Fortunately, she didn't seem upset, more like entertained. "Roscoe the houseplant has some odd rules for visitors."

I repositioned on the love seat, my legs under me, so I could face her. Might as well go to the next level since my mouth had already gotten me to this point. "He has standards and respects openness."

"As he should. Always."

"Are you just saying that?"

"What happened to trusting me?" Imogen placed a hand on her chest.

"I do, but even from our short time together, I know your family is a sensitive subject."

She snorted. "You've only known me for a day, yet you understand so much about me."

"I'd like to understand you even more."

"Me too." She didn't call me out on dropping the Roscoe ruse, as flimsy as it was.

"Good. Now that we got that settled, what's next on the agenda of getting to know each other?"

"That's a very good question. So far, I've learned

you like Portobello Road. You have a lovely singing voice. You've never had a pet. You're an accountant. You name things. From the shirt you wore earlier, your team is the Denver Broncos."

"How do you know the Broncos?"

"We've heard of the NFL here. Some American friends of mine throw a Super Bowl party every year. I think they won a few years ago."

"Color me impressed." I circled a finger in front of my face.

She bonked her head. "Oh, your favorite movies are *Notting Hill* and *Bedknobs and Broomsticks*. How'd I almost forget those? Is there anything else I should know?"

"Oh, you have no idea how much goes on inside here." I pointed to my head. "And, here." I placed a hand over my heart.

She gulped her water.

"Why did the mention of Paris scare you away?"

"It didn't." When I started to protest, she added, "That's what scared me away."

I blinked. Then again. "I think you're going to have to explain that."

"I wanted to jump on a train right then with you. Knowing that did my head in." She cupped the back of her head. "I needed time to process it."

"Let me see if I'm getting this straight. You bailed after lunch because you want to run away with me to

Paris. So instead of running with me, you ran from me?"

"Exactly."

"That's the nicest thing I've heard all day. Maybe ever."

CHAPTER TWENTY-ONE

"If that's the nicest thing you've heard, then you have a very low bar." She laughed, shaking her head, placing her hand only a few feet above ground level.

I swatted her hand, resulting with it brushing her thigh on the follow-through, a surge of electricity crackling in the air. "Quite the opposite. I have a very high bar."

The creases around her eyes furrowed, which I was noticing was a common occurrence for her. "I'm not following your logic."

"The fact that you freaked yourself out about an overnight trip shows me it wouldn't have been just an overnight thing. Not that I think it equates to getting married but rather to the possibility of getting to know each other with the intention of laying a foundation." I waved a hand in front of my face. "Never mind. Forget I said any of that."

"I can't and don't want to."

I expected her to leap to her feet and bound out the door. Or would she take the shortcut through the open and unscreened window? Her escape after lunch wasn't dramatic, but would two episodes in one day cause her to chip away some of her reserve?

She seemed to wait for me to say something, but I had no idea what to say without digging the *grave of what could've been* deeper.

An odd smile appeared on her face, and she continued to hold her tongue.

I squirmed, playing with the string on my shorts. "Are you trying to drive me crazy?" I finally asked.

"No, but you get this adorable expression when you think you've upset me."

"I haven't?"

"Nope."

"But earlier—you bailed. Why aren't you bailing now?" I looked at her and then back to the open window.

She followed my eyes, chuckling. "Are you picturing me jumping through the window?"

"Kinda, yeah."

Her body rumbled with laughter.

Mine started to shake as well.

After a few moments of hilarity, she asked, "You haven't had much luck with relationships, have you?"

I shook my head. "I never really got serious with anyone, but today has shown me I can be a bit intense right from the start. This is a whole new revelation."

She bobbed her head thoughtfully, and I was really starting to like how she took her time to let things sit while not flipping out when I did the exact opposite. What had Jane said? Yin and yang?

"You?" I asked.

"I have a hard time letting someone in. Hence why you're thinking I'm going to jump through a window. You seem to have an uncanny ability to pick up on my thoughts." She raised a finger. "I never considered the window, though."

"Well, I did also factor in the door option for your escape. I thought jumping out a window would be really low on your list of things to add to life experiences."

"It would make a great story, wouldn't it?" Her eyes shone with possibilities, making me think she did like adding experiences but after thought.

"A memorable one at that. Especially if we ended up working out and I could say, *You know, in the beginning Immie was so afraid of getting to know me she jumped through a window like Superwoman.*"

"My running away instead of dashing to your rescue negates the Superwoman comparison, doesn't it?"

"Right." I nodded. "This is good. We're communicating. Getting things said."

"It is." She gazed at me, and I wanted to know what it'd feel like to kiss her. Was that what the sparkle in her eyes conveyed? Kiss me?

I stared back at her, making my best effort to telepathically scream: *Kiss me right now or...* I had no idea what type of threat accompanied the action, but her full lips seemed to be pulling me closer.

Imogen's head leaned toward the middle of the love seat.

I started to laugh.

She pulled back. "What?"

"We're sitting on a love seat."

She looked down at the beige fabric. "And?"

"I've never had a first kiss on a love seat. I mean, really. Has anyone?"

"In all of history, I'd wager yes." She eyed the furniture again. "While this doesn't actually qualify, since it's not shaped in an S, this type of furniture, in history, has been referred to as a courting or kissing bench. The S shape was meant to provide some type of barrier, since the couple would have to lean to make contact."

"I love that you know that. Who knows details like that?"

"Me, I guess."

"You really do love trivia night at the pub, don't you?"

Her cheeks turned a lovely shade of pink.

"I, for one, am glad it's not actually in an S shape."

"Yes, it wouldn't fit so nicely into this space if it was. And if you wanted to stretch out while watching telly, well, you wouldn't be able to. Not comfortably, at least."

God, she was adorable. The type of cuteness that absolutely required kissing. I leaned forward. She did the same. Inch by inch, our mouths came closer.

CHAPTER TWENTY-TWO

Before contact, we both stopped, but we were close enough if I stuck my tongue out, I'd be able to taste her lips. She gazed intently at me, her blue eyes smoldering with desire. It was fucking hot and an intensity I'd never been on the receiving end of.

She smiled, not pulling back.

Every nerve ending in my body fired to *damn the torpedoes* level.

We moved closer.

Our mouths met, her lips soft and inviting.

Feeling hers against mine pleased me more than I would have thought possible. I'd felt a bond with her since the start, but now that there was a physical connection, everything came full circle, wrapping comforting tendrils around my heart. All of my time on this earth, I'd been absolutely terrified to put it at risk and had never given my heart or myself a chance to experience the full throttle of life.

Her tongue eased inside my mouth, not with hesitancy but tenderness. I welcomed it, melting into her embrace, her arms luring me further into the moment.

My arms found her, pulling her into my orbit as well, wanting to give everything I had to her and to receive everything from Imogen. How was this happening? Why was this happening? I'd been so clear how my time in London would go. Work and travel. Now there was this wrinkle, and fuck, I loved it.

The kiss kicked up a notch, knocking the how and why out of my head, so the only thought left was *wowzers*!

We continued to rev the intensity, until Imogen pulled away to catch her breath. "If you were going to name a female dog, what would you name it?"

"Clemmie," I said, trying to recover from the lack of oxygen.

"Short for Clementine?"

I nodded, sipping my water.

"That's perfect." She ran a finger down the side of my face. "You're perfect."

"I thought we discussed this. Perfection is a terrible thing to chase or to ascribe to someone."

She brushed her fingers across my swollen lips. "I think there are different definitions. You weren't a good fit for Jane, making you imperfect."

"Or normal. Jane is in a category all her own." I pressed my forehead to hers.

Imogen laughed. "Ask me a question."

"If you were planning a once-in-a-lifetime trip, what destination would you choose?"

"Africa. Botswana specifically."

I yanked my head away. "Jane prepped you well."

Imogen narrowed her eyes. "I'm not sure what to make of that."

"She told you I've always wanted to visit Botswana. To go on game drives. Drink wine with giraffes silhouetted against the setting sun." I stared off dreamily into space.

"Check this out." She tapped her phone and displayed a photo that showed exactly what I'd described about giraffes and sunset. "A friend of mine went there last year and had an amazing time. Ever since seeing her photos, I've yearned to go."

"I was probably the only kid who looked forward to dentist appointments, because I loved looking through *National Geographic* magazines."

"I've been subscribing for twenty years now."

"You still get it?"

"The digital version."

Our foreheads met again.

"Maybe Jane was right," I said.

"Maybe."

"You don't sound convinced."

"It's not that. I'm simply looking forward to peeling back more layers."

"Speaking of layers…" I left the rest unsaid.

She cupped my cheek. "Yes?"

"Do you have to be anywhere first thing in the morning?"

"Nope. I'm hoping to take someone I know for breakfast in the morning. One she'll like."

"Do I know this someone?" Even though I knew the answer, I still held my breath.

"You might."

"Describe her to me."

"Well, she's American. So, pushy and loud with no filter."

"Gawd, I hate those types."

"They're a breed of their own, but she's also intelligent and has the most adorable dimple right here." She pressed her finger to my right cheek. "Her sense of humor keeps me on my toes. Sometimes, I don't know if she's teasing or being honest."

"Is it possible for both to be true?"

"I think so, or I hope that's the case, because it's the part of her that keeps pulling me in."

"What else?" I pressed.

"She's a great kisser." She gave me a peck on the lips.

"That's very important. There's nothing worse than a bad kiss."

"I think all of my kissing up until fairly recently has been a disappointment, but I didn't know it."

"I might be in the same boat, but we'll need more data."

She chuckled. "Data, huh?"

"Yes. Care to conduct a science experiment with me?"

"That's one of her things. Putting things in such an odd way it's charming."

"Lucky for her."

"Why's that?"

"Because she'd hate not being able to do this again." I kissed her.

CHAPTER TWENTY-THREE

AFTER ANOTHER EPIC ROUND OF KISSING, WE both came up for air.

Taking a sip of water, Imogen looked around the apartment. "Where's your bedroom?"

"You're in it."

She looked over both shoulders, inspecting the love seat. "You don't have to sleep on this, do you? It's not long enough."

I pointed to the closet doors that housed the murphy bed.

The deepening of her furrowed brow was proof I hadn't cleared up her confusion.

"Let me show you." I got up and pulled the two doors open, folding them to the side and then lowering the bed.

"Oh, goodness. I knew your place was tiny, but I hadn't figured it was this tiny."

I moved to the windows and shut the curtains completely, pulling one back briefly. "Night, night, Roscoe."

"Is the bed comfortable?" She wore a dubious expression.

"I've only used it once, but I have to admit I was surprised by how well I slept last night. Of course, it was after a day of getting through immigration with my visa and rushing to the apartment to let the movers in. It was an action-packed and stressful day. Maybe tonight will be the true test."

"I should get going and let you find out." She didn't move a muscle.

"Remember my need to collect data?"

She nodded.

"In order to give a full verdict of the murphy bed, I think I need to put the mattress to the test—not solely the sleeping data point."

She continued nodding, clearly processing what I was saying, but perhaps not wanting to jinx things, she stayed quiet.

I hopped onto the bed and started jumping. "It's a good thing I'm in the basement, or this might annoy my new neighbors."

She tilted her head. "I think you should be aware the bed lifts a little bit when you bound into the air, but it's holding up."

I beckoned her with a finger. "Come on. I need lots and lots of data."

"You want me to hop on the bed with you?" she asked, sounding completely floored by the request.

"You know you want to."

She folded her arms across her chest.

I planted my feet and waved both hands, insisting she join me.

She stared me down.

Evidently, she needed some motivation. "I'll take off my top if you join me."

She blew out a raspberry. "That's flat-out bribery."

"Not seeing the problem from your end." I hefted up the hem of my shirt a bit, giving her a peek.

Her resolve started to waver.

"I bet when you woke up this morning, you had no idea your day would include an American asking you to jump up and down to test out her Murphy bed."

"Nothing like this has ever happened to me."

"Me either." I laughed. "It's a whole new adventure." I started jumping again. "Please, join me."

I could see her stiff shoulders loosening.

"I might take off more than my shirt."

"I can't be bought." Her smile screamed she could.

"You can take your top off, too." I got more air with my last jump, the bed lifting a bit higher. "I need you, or I may get hurt."

"Now you're resorting to blackmail. Do you have a bottom?"

"American, remember?" I turned around, still

hopping. "To answer your question, I do have a bottom." I spanked my runner's bum.

I felt movement on the bed and turned around.

She grinned self-consciously.

"You are up for adventure tonight."

"Is that what you call this?"

"One hop and you'll get your reward." I grabbed the lower portion of my shirt.

"Is this how you are on all of your dates?"

"Has this been a date?"

"A blind one, I'd say."

"Earlier, yes. But, then you came over to my apartment on your own accord. Didn't you?"

She nodded.

"That's your favorite form of communication. Nodding." I took her hands into mine. "On the count of three, jump with me."

She pursed her lips, or was she trying not to smile?

"One. Two." I gave her hands a supportive squeeze. "Three!"

We jumped together, the bed lifting dangerously off the floor, causing me to laugh, while Imogen looked at the mattress below us and then at the wall, as if calculating whether or not we were about to be smashed into it.

I steadied my feet and hoisted my shirt over my head. "I play fair."

"I see that." She swallowed, her eyes staying on

mine, but they flicked downward, not once but twice. She swallowed again.

"Oh, I promised you more for inducement, didn't I?"

Imogen remained frozen.

I put my arms around her neck, pulling her a step closer. "Will a kiss be a good start?"

She didn't remain inactive this time, planting her lips hungrily on mine.

My hand slid under her shirt, wanting to know what it'd feel like to touch her. As if she was reading my mind, she removed her top, tossing it over her shoulder. I didn't know she had that move in her, but it promised she had even more incredible ones.

We lowered onto the bed, with her on top of me, still kissing, while one of her hands trailed down my side.

"Shall we commence the final test for the bed?" I asked.

"The final? I don't think we've even begun to put this mattress through enough rigorous testing."

I smirked. "I like the sound of that."

CHAPTER TWENTY-FOUR

"Glad to hear it." Imogen took the reins, dispatching my shorts.

My breath hitched.

Her fingers trekked over my panties.

I quirked one eyebrow. "Are those staying?"

"For the moment." She cupped my pussy. "Does jumping always get you so hot?"

"Depends on my partner."

"Is that right?" She eased the silky fabric down my legs. "Oh, it really does turn you on."

I glanced down, spying a shimmer on the inside of my thigh.

"I don't like to do things by half measure."

She grinned. "I'm taking a lot of mental notes, FYI."

"Good. You're the one who said there are many more ways to test the bed."

"You love data. A lot." She kissed her way down the inside of my right thigh, past my calf, raising my foot, and explored my toes with her mouth, causing me to moan. Then her fingers walked up and down my other leg, tickling me.

"I didn't know legs could get this tan."

"I spent a couple of weeks hiking in the Rocky Mountains before moving here."

"That would explain the tan line." She wrapped her fingers around one of my ankles.

"Do tan lines get you hot? I have more."

"I've noticed that." Her mouth began the trek up my left leg, stopping at the demarcation between tan and pale. "I doubt your tan will last long here."

"It never did in Boston either."

Imogen continued moving up, taking in a deep breath when she arrived at my pussy. Seeming pleased by the scent, she gulped in another lungful.

My hips moved to pull Imogen where I wanted her.

"Losing the control battle?"

"I'm blaming you."

"I'll take it." She didn't bother trying to curb the smirk from forming on her face. Her hand split my lips, giving her access to slowly insert a finger inside.

I exhaled sharply but wanted much more.

Imogen added another finger, moving up to kiss me. My muscles constricted around her, while my tongue greeted hers in a *fuck me* way. She cranked her wrist to give her more room to go in and out, deeper and deeper, while we kissed.

My nails scored her back.

Without having to voice my urgent need, Imogen gave me one last, passionate kiss before her mouth started its trek southward, her fingers still moving in and out of me.

Her mouth landed on my right nipple, teasing the hardening bud and biting down on it with exactly the right pressure. My need grew with each passing second. Not that Imogen seemed to notice, or perhaps she did, because she released a sexy growl.

After paying attention to my other nipple, she continued moving downward, leaving a pleasing trail of kisses.

Arriving at the belly button, she kissed the sensitive flesh around it, dipping her tongue into the small depression.

Still moving down, she raked my pubic hair, while her fingers dove in deep.

She made it past the hair, arriving at my clit, and it practically stood up as if saying, "If you don't pay me attention, I'll shrivel up and die."

"You feel so good," I purred, fisting her hair.

Imogen increased the intensity of easing in and out. Her tongue concentrated on my clit, her eyes meeting mine, showing how much she enjoyed my desperate gyrations and heavy breathing. With each flick of her tongue, I became wetter and wetter, the slapping sound of her hand more prominent in the small room. How she was able to keep her mouth in the right spot despite my jouncing about on the mattress was testament to her commitment to a job well done.

Both of our labored breathing quickened, and I was so close to exploding.

Her fingers moved in deep, and my nails dug into her firm shoulders.

My legs started to spasm, the sign I was about to come. Imogen dove in deeper, holding her fingers on my magic spot, and that set off a wave of ecstasy. Her mouth didn't let up, lapping my clit.

My body started to tremble as I uttered, "Holy fuck!"

A second wave started to crest, and Imogen slowed her fingers and tongue, giving me time to enjoy the sensation.

Even with Imogen trying to slow things down, my body had a mind of its own, and an orgasm ripped through me.

"Oh, Jesus!"

I came hard.

Neither of us moved for many moments, both gathering our strength and breath.

She climbed on top of me, her weight pressing me delightfully into the mattress.

"Well, the bed passed yet another test," I panted.

"It sure did." Her breath was warm on the crook of my neck.

"Never again will I say a bad word about Murphy beds."

She chuckled, still laboring to breathe. "All of them or just this one?"

"Good point. We may have to test all of them."

"In the world or only the ones in London?"

"Let's keep putting this one through the wringer." I pulled her mouth to mine.

In one rapid movement, I rolled her onto her back. "You still have your jeans on. How is that possible?"

"You didn't take them off."

"Not a mistake I intend to live with." I removed all of the remaining articles.

"I need your lips. Kiss me."

She didn't have to ask twice.

Imogen hesitated briefly when my fingers separated the lips below and found their way inside.

My mouth tugged on her earlobe, eliciting an excited moan. My tongue dove inside her ear, being met with another wave of pleasing moans.

My tongue traveled down her body, delighting to land on sensitive spots, causing Imogen to writhe excitedly underneath me.

When I arrived at her clit, taking it into my mouth, she nearly bucked off the bed. I circled her bud, pulling Imogen closer and closer to release.

She gripped the sides of my head.

My fingers and mouth didn't let up.

I gazed into her stunning blue eyes, the color deepening like the middle of the ocean, but she was unable to keep them open, and her body quivered, causing me to up my efforts to get her over the finish line.

CHAPTER TWENTY-FIVE

THERE WAS A RUMBLE OF A TRUCK IDLING outside, followed by Nigel yelling. I groaned, pulling a pillow over my head.

"Does the man stand outside all morning waiting for truck drivers to yell at?" I grumbled.

"What man?"

I bolted up in bed, clutching the sheet to my chest.

"Are you okay?" Imogen sat up, placing a hand on my back.

I looked over my shoulder sheepishly. "Oh, yeah. I'm fine. It's... I kinda forgot you stayed the night. Morning isn't my best time."

"I disagree. I seem to remember having a very enjoyable time around midnight, or was it closer to one?"

"That doesn't count as morning to me. This"—I flicked a hand in the air to the sliver of sunlight streaming through a crack in the curtains—"is legitimately morning." I yawned.

"Poor you. But who's the yeller?"

"My landlord. When I met him, he seemed like such a charming man in an adorable mismatched tweed suit. I'm learning that's how he cons people into thinking he's harmless."

She stretched her arms overhead. "A rookie mistake being taken in by an old British chap."

"Is the threat rampant?" I gave her side eye but ended up stifling another yawn.

She laid back down onto her side and propped up her face. "They're a danger to the world. Did he have a brolly?"

"What's that?"

She rolled her eyes like I was so naïve. "Clearly, I can't let you fend for yourself. Not in a city filled with old men wielding umbrellas." Her expression turned frightened. "He didn't have a pocket watch in his vest, did he?"

"Not that I remember." I closed one eye, trying to recall but couldn't. "Why?"

She widened her eyes. "The ones with pocket watches belong to a gang going back to the Victorian age. Those individuals should never be messed with."

"Are you talking about watches on a chain?" I couldn't understand how something so out of date would be a gang symbol.

She nodded.

"That's the weirdest gang sign. Who'd be afraid of Nigel? I'm learning he likes to yell at truck drivers, but—wait! He did say the man would regret his actions or something like that." I tried to remember his exact wording, but it'd happened before I had coffee, so the chances were slim. "You don't think he called someone to do anything to the poor guy, do you?" I ran a hand over my throat, meaning murder.

Imogen burst into laughter.

"You're fucking with me, aren't you?" I slapped her, not hard at all, and left my hand resting on her hip.

"I couldn't help it. I enjoy your confused puppy face."

"I can't believe you. Taking advantage of my lack of coffee."

"What were you picturing? A hoard of old men rampaging the city with brollies, always consulting the time so as not to miss their afternoon tea?" Imogen sat up to act out old men bent over with age.

"That's not a pretty image." I pinched my eyes shut. "Let's move on to something else."

"Come here." She rolled onto her back and held her arm out for me to snuggle. "Let me protect you from the evils in this big bad city."

"I'd be more trusting if you hadn't played me for a fool." I still rested my head on her shoulder, wrapping an arm around her midsection, because how could I stay mad at such a gorgeous woman naked in my bed?

"I don't think you're holding it against me, or is this a protest cuddle?"

"You're surprisingly easy to cuddle with." I sank into the feeling.

"Lucky me."

"What time is it?"

I felt her hitch a shoulder. "Does it matter?"

"No, I guess not. I'm wondering if we have time to fall back asleep."

"It's Sunday. We can stay in bed all day." She ran her hand down my back.

"I like you on Sunday mornings, aside from the teasing, but I'm sure I'll appreciate being played the fool after coffee." I yawned.

"Does that mean you don't or won't like me the other six days of the week?"

"No idea yet. I'll let you know." I started to drift off, enjoying her holding me tighter.

∽

THE MATTRESS LURCHED to the side, and I slowly opened my eyes.

Imogen, fully clothed and with a cup of coffee in each hand, gazed down at me. "There's a coffee shop on the corner."

"You left and came back?"

"Yep. You'd be really easy to burgle."

"Burgle." I laughed. "Somehow, that sounds faintly charming. Not like back home."

"What do you guys call it?" She drank her coffee.

"Technically, it should be burglarized, but I think most use robbed because it's easier to say. Have you been burgled?" The word still made me chuckle, but I already preferred it to the American way.

"Seven times."

"Yeah, right. Not falling for that after the old-man gang." I sipped my coffee. "Jesus, I needed this. Thank you."

"I really have been burgled that many times. It's why I moved out of Tooting to Earl's Court."

"Is Earl's Court safer?"

"So far, so good." She crossed her fingers.

"Will I need extra locks or something?" I eyed the large windows, which could be used as an entrance, and they didn't have screens, making it that much easier.

"I doubt it. Nigel keeps a close eye on the comings and goings."

"Is he still outside?"

"He watched me from his shop. Luckily, I didn't see a pocket watch, so he's not a menace. To you, but I don't recommend getting a truck."

"I don't even have a license anymore. I never drove in Boston, and mine expired a week before I moved here. Besides, you guys drive on the wrong side of the road."

"We drive on the proper side." Her shoulders stiffened, but I think that was for show.

"No, Americans drive on the right side of the road in both respects."

"What do you mean?"

"We drive on the correct side, which literally happens to be on the right-hand side."

She grinned at me over her coffee. "Is that what you want to discuss?"

"I've found those on the losing side usually try to change the topic."

"Or the person doesn't see the point in arguing with a crazy." She made the universal sign that I had bats in the belfry.

I exaggerated an eye roll and blew out a frustrated breath. "While I like you getting up to get coffee, there is one problem."

"What's that?"

"You're dressed and not in bed."

"That could be easily fixed, you know."

"Is that right?"

Nigel screaming at something outside made us turn our heads to the curtained windows.

"Or, you could get dressed, and we could go somewhere more peaceful for breakfast. If I remember correctly, you require regular feeding."

My stomach grumbled. I looked down at it. "Traitor."

She smirked victoriously.

"I don't see why you're gloating. I had a certain bedroom activity in mind."

"I like being right, just like I was when we were discussing driving on the proper side of the road."

"So much for not arguing with crazy." I drank heavily from my coffee. "Did you shower?"

She shook her head slowly, understanding seeping into those mesmerizing blue eyes.

"Do you guys use the proverb, *Kill two birds with one stone?*"

Imogen tipped her head back, laughing. "Are all American women so charming?"

"Not sure about all of us, but I'm charming as hell." I finished my coffee. "Let's get wet."

CHAPTER TWENTY-SIX

In the bathroom, I stripped down and cranked the water on. In under a minute, I saw steam and tested the water. Stepping into the bathtub, which was much higher than I was used to, I shouted, "Are you coming?"

The bathroom door opened and then closed. "It might take more than screaming to get me to orgasm."

"I really hope so, because I have big plans for this small space."

Imogen craned her neck around the shower curtain. "It's not as bad as some flats I've been in. And, luckily for you, it's spotless. Nigel may be a crazed old-man unwilling to let go of colonialism, but he's a neat-freak racist."

"Neat and racist don't go together, ever. Strip, please." I batted my eyelashes.

She pursed her lips but followed my directions.

The stream of hot water brought me fully back to life. "I could never live without a shower."

"Do you plan on sharing?"

I pulled her under the water with me. "Better?"

She kissed me, the water streaming down on us.

"It's like kissing under a waterfall, but no slippery rocks or creatures below us." I squirted citrus shower gel onto a mesh sponge I'd purchased yesterday. "Where should I start?"

"The beginning."

"Is that code for front or back?"

"Dealer's choice."

I motioned for her to twirl around, taking care of her creamy skin, paying extra attention to her scrumptious ass. "Are you a runner?"

"Yes."

I eyed her firm calves. "I run, but I have to force myself to do it every time. I'm successful about four days a week."

"If you need help with motivation, you can join my running club."

"Running club?"

"You'll find they're quite popular in the parks here. You can tell one is coming by the music."

"Does one of them cart a boom box or something?" I continued sponging her body, ensuring her breasts were properly washed.

"Pretty much. I think there are running groups that

also stop for short history lessons. Wouldn't an American like that? Killing two birds?" she teased.

"I may be passionate about checking off things on my to-do list, but that might be a step too far."

"I do think running with others helps. Or it does with me." She made a show of checking out my lower half. "But, what you're doing now is working."

"Thank you." I hunched down. "Wouldn't want to neglect this part."

Her chest hitched. "Please don't."

I skimmed my tongue along the inside of her freshly washed thigh, briefly flicking her clit.

Imogen placed a hand on my head, steadying herself, the water flowing over her body and onto me. Looking up, I smiled, pulling some hair out of my mouth.

I snaked upward and wrapped my arms around her neck for a kiss.

Imogen stepped into it, pushing me against the side of the shower, her leg separating mine.

I ran my thumb over her bottom lip.

She reached down and entered me.

I bit her bottom lip while she added another finger inside me, moving them in and out.

We continued kissing, but Imogen didn't let up, pumping her wrist, going in and out, her urgency matching my own. I rested my head against the wall, and she took one of my nipples into her mouth, the shower water hitting her back, but only the occasional droplet hit my face, the rest of me shielded by Imogen.

Her teeth clamped down on my other nipple, while her free hand caressed the back of my head, her fingers still working magic down below.

"Oh, Jesus, don't stop!" I exclaimed.

She didn't and pumped her fingers even more.

I wrapped my arms tightly around Imogen, my mouth seeking hers. When the lights started to flicker behind my eyelids, I accidentally bit her lip much harder than I intended.

Either not noticing or ignoring the action, Imogen dove in deep, holding it just right, releasing a guttural, "Oh fuck!" from me.

My legs shook.

Imogen pushed in deeper, initiating yet another wave of bliss, while pressing my body against the wall, probably in an effort to keep me on my feet.

As the tremors subsided some, she said, "I think we got dirty instead of clean."

"Sorry but not sorry." I opened my eyes. "Your turn."

CHAPTER TWENTY-SEVEN

I STOOD IN THE MIDDLE OF THE MAIN ROOM, holding a hair dryer in one hand and the cord on the other. "There isn't a plug in the bathroom."

"Yeah, that's not a thing here." She slipped one leg into her jeans.

"Plugs or hair dryers?"

"Plugs in the bathroom." She slanted her head to inspect the appliance. "It looks like that's a UK plug, so you should be good."

"I picked it up at Boots on my way home yesterday. I was surprised the store doesn't sell shoes at all. I wasn't able to dry my hair yesterday because I hadn't picked up one yet. I thought my GPS was messing with me when I typed in *pharmacy near me* and three Boots popped up."

She zipped up her jeans. "I think the founder was named James Boot. Or was it John?" She motioned to a plug near the desk in the corner. "You can plug it in there."

"But, there's no mirror." I spun around helplessly. "The only mirror is in the bathroom."

She gave me a quizzical look as if trying to find soothing words but failing.

"Are you saying no bathrooms in the UK have plugs for hair dryers?" I held it like the device was a delicate baby.

"Basically."

"Where do you dry your hair?"

"In the kitchen."

I blinked.

She put a hand on each of my shoulders. "It's going to be okay. Millions of people in this country are able to get ready in the morning."

"I didn't realize how barbaric the conditions would be."

She laughed. "Come on. I googled a breakfast place I think you'll like."

"I do like breakfast."

"Not British flapjacks, though." She jerked her head to the plug. "Be brave."

"You know, I think I'll let it air-dry again."

"It worked for you yesterday." She waggled her brows in a seductive way.

"Good to know." I stared at the hair dryer in my hands. "The kitchen? Really?"

"Do I need to prove it?"

"Does that mean I can come over?"

"To dry your hair? That seems extreme."

"Very funny." I placed the hair dryer on the antique desk crammed into the corner by the window and then opened the blinds. "Good morning, Roscoe. Do you need a drink of water?" I tipped some water from the bottle that sat on the desk. Turning back around, I asked, "Honestly, how many things are going to cause my brain to melt down?"

"Luckily for you, you've been able to get past the *no plugs in the bathroom* and flapjacks debacles. You're such an experienced world traveler who lets the water roll off your back." She shimmied.

I laughed but still said, "I remember all the way back to yesterday when you didn't mock me this much."

"You got to know me. It opened the floodgates." She shrugged, pulling on a T-shirt I gave her since she only had the clothes she wore yesterday.

I wrapped my arms around her neck. "I like it."

"Sarcasm gets you hot." She ran a finger down the side of my face.

"Intelligence and playfulness are *major* turn-ons." I emphasized major.

"Good news for me." She gave me a quick peck. "Do you have a Tube pass?"

"Yeah. My relo person loaded one for me."

She pressed her hands together. "Let's rock and roll, then."

"Do we need brollies? I love that word."

"Pretty soon you'll be talking like a Brit. But why do we need them? Are you afraid of Nigel?"

"Jane said it's supposed to lash rain—her words—today." I looked out the window but could only see feet in sandals or flip-flops.

"About that. Rain isn't in the forecast for the next seven days."

"Jane lied?"

"Shocking news."

"I should be mad at her and you for not correcting her—"

"You didn't speak up when she said you missed your dog." She wagged a gotcha finger.

"Okay, okay." I motioned to Imogen. "It seems to be working out in both our favors."

"Apparently, Jane was on to something." She kissed my cheek.

∽

IMOGEN OPENED the door to the restaurant and waved for me to go in.

"Oh my god." I twirled around. "This is amazing!"

She grinned.

"It has red stools, Formica tables, and black and white checkered floors. Just like an American diner back home."

"That was my goal. I think it's best if we baby-step

you into the British way of life. I mean, the hair dryer incident is proof you're fragile." She bumped my side with her elbow.

A hostess led us to a booth.

I skimmed the menu, breaking into a broad smile when I zoomed in on the buttermilk pancake options. "Do you like anything on the menu?"

She laughed, placing her cheek on her palm. "Americans don't own breakfast, you know. I'll get an omelet."

"There's wine, beer, and cocktails on the breakfast menu." I looked up at her. "Points to Britain for that."

"Are you going to get one?"

I shook my head. "I might hold off for the pub."

"Wise choice. Since it's a beautiful day, I have one in mind."

"The friar one you mentioned yesterday?"

"No, across the river. We can get a beer and sit near the water."

"That sounds nice." I tried making eye contact with anyone to place our order, but none of the employees looked in our direction. "Are you sure you're okay spending the day with me?"

"Like I said earlier, I can't let you fend for yourself in this barbaric country."

"Is that the only reason?"

"That's for me to know and for you to find out." The left side of her mouth curled up in a sexy way.

Finally, a server arrived and took our orders, not wasting a second on chitchat.

"So, why no plugs in the bathrooms?"

"It's not safe." She scrunched her brow. "Plugs have to be three meters away from the bath or shower."

"That's what…?" I pinched my eyes shut, remembering the difference between the US and metric system. "Over nine feet."

"I think so."

"If that's the case, every bathroom I've had in the US has been a deadly hazard, yet I'm still breathing." I ran a hand up and down in the air to prove I was indeed alive and well.

"Why do Americans have such little regard for human life?" She smirked.

"You're joking, but not respecting life is a major problem in the US. That, however, is a conversation for another day. I'm not big on mixing politics and Sunday mornings."

From her expression, she seemed much relieved.

A surly dude placed our coffees down, along with a bowl of creamers. I selected two for mine, while Imogen grabbed one along with two sugar packets.

I held my cup with both hands right below my chin. "This feels natural, doesn't it?"

"What?"

"Having breakfast together."

"It does." She smiled.

"I'm glad I met you."

Our food arrived, and my pancakes looked gloriously American. "And, I'm super-duper happy you found this place." I drenched my stack of four with maple syrup. Chewing the first bite, I moaned in delight.

"That sounds like an endorsement."

"This might have to become a Sunday tradition."

"Starting a tradition so soon. That has to be a good sign for your adjustment to London." She forked in a bite of her grilled mushroom omelet.

"What does it say about me that I want to come to an American diner every Sunday?" I prepped another forkful, bigger than the last now that I knew it wouldn't disappoint.

"You're human and want things the way you're used to."

After washing down the bite with coffee, I asked, "What's your favorite breakfast?"

"The full English."

I waved for her to fill me in.

"Sausage, rashers, beans, toast, tomatoes, and mushrooms."

"What kind of beans?" I crinkled my nose in disgust.

"Baked beans."

"With breakfast?" I asked much too loudly.

"It's yummy." She rubbed her belly. "Beans and toast are a staple here."

"From the outside, you people seem so civilized, but I'm learning you aren't." I loaded my fork. "Baked beans are for BBQs with brats. Not breakfast. Yuck!"

"I plan to convert you." She jabbed her fork at me.

"Best of luck with that one." I made a gagging noise.

"Careful, or I won't take you to the pub after this."

"Fine. I'll do my best to refrain from telling you how wrong you are about absolutely everything."

"Off to a good start!" Her gorgeous eyes met mine, and I had to agree. We were.

CHAPTER TWENTY-EIGHT

We sat on a wall outside of the pub, our feet dangling over the side facing the Thames, the sunlight glittering on the water.

"I can't believe I'm here, having a pint, while staring at St. Paul's Cathedral across the river." I held out my arm. "Pinch me."

She didn't, taking a sip of her beer instead, giving me her trademark *don't be silly* smile.

"Do you know how lucky you are?"

"What do you mean?" She gazed at me curiously.

"You live in this amazing city." I waved my hand to the mix of old and new architecture across the way. "Look at it."

Her eyes swept the horizon. *"When a man is tired of London, he is tired of life."*

"Who said that?"

"You don't believe I came up with it on the spot?" She slowly swiveled her face back to mine.

"No way. A man had to have said that."

"You're correct. Samuel Johnson." She poked my leg with a finger.

"I could sit here all day."

"We can, as long as both of us don't get up at the same time. Watch out for pushy American tourists. They love to steal the best seats in the house." She cracked a beautiful smile. "Or sit at a table for four when there's only one of them."

"Oh, Americans are absolutely the worst!"

"Loud."

"Obnoxious."

"Good in bed," she tossed in, taking me by surprise.

I nearly choked on my beer. "Is that right?"

She nodded enthusiastically.

"What's your sample size?"

She mimed her lips were sealed.

"That's not fair!" I nudged my shoulder into hers.

"How many Brits have you shagged?"

"Since arriving?" I hedged.

"See. You don't want to answer either." She waggled a finger at me.

"Well, it's possibly a touchy subject between us."

She narrowed her eyes.

"I dated Jane." I returned her gaze to convey the import of that statement.

"Ah, so did I. Now I see where you're going."

I shivered. "That's weird to think about. Let's talk about something else."

"Such as?"

"Anything that doesn't involve shagging the same woman, but I would like it noted I like the word shagging. Possibly even more than brolly."

She gave me a knowing look. "Hmm... how about we discuss Winston Churchill?"

"No men."

"So, we can't talk about women we've slept with or men?" She held two fingers in the air. "What does that leave?"

"What's your favorite television show?"

"I like crime shows."

I cranked my neck practically at light speed toward her. "Really?"

"That surprises you?"

"I would've pegged you for a historical drama fan. *Gentleman Jack* or along those lines." A seagull swooped low over the water.

"Occasionally, but I prefer *Vera* or *Shetland*."

"I loooove *Shetland*." I added more Os to love and continued to enthuse, "His Scottish accent is so charming, and it cracks me up every time he says *murder*. I never knew the word could make me smile, but each time makes me happy, and when he says *murder inquiry*, I grin ear to ear." I demonstrated for her and repeated it.

She playfully looked at her watch. "Oh, I forgot I have an appointment."

"Nice try. You've already told me Sundays are just for you."

"And, here I sit with you."

"That's even better than the Scottish pronunciation of murder."

"Mur-der," she said in an exaggerated Scottish accent.

"Why didn't you say that last night in bed?"

Her shoulders rumbled with laughter. "I'll remember it for next time."

"There's going to be a next time?"

She looked deeply into my eyes. "Oh, I think so."

"What are you doing for dinner?"

"What would you like to do?"

That response filled me with joy, but I tried to play it cool. "I happen to know a lovely Italian restaurant close to my place."

"Didn't you have that last night with Jane?"

"I did and went gaga for their blue cheese pasta."

"Pasta," she said, stressing the first syllable, not second like I was accustomed.

"Oh, that's another keeper for later tonight."

"Blue cheese pasta?"

"Pronouncing it that way. Say it with murder."

"You're insane."

"I am. It's probably time you know that." I raised a hand. "Before you say anything, I have no plans to change. It's taken me nearly decades to accept myself, and now that I have, others have to deal with it."

"That's good, because I like you the way you are." She pressed my nose with her finger.

"Aw, that's the nicest thing you've said."

"Nicer than when I said the thought of Paris freaked me out?"

"Yes. Do you plan to keep getting more and more adorable?" I made goo-goo eyes at her.

"I'm just being me." She hefted a shoulder.

"We're both being ourselves, and we've only known each other for twenty-four hours, which makes me wonder how long this will last."

She got to her feet.

"Way to pop my balloon so suddenly."

"We need another round, silly." She tapped the seat where she'd been sitting. "Don't let anyone steal my spot. Especially not an American."

CHAPTER TWENTY-NINE

It was roughly four in the afternoon, and we made our way through Kensington Gardens after walking from the river.

"Thanks for walking back with me."

"My pleasure." She slipped her hand into mine. "This is my normal Sunday. Wandering through the city. I'll admit having you with me has made this particular Sunday one of the best."

"Excuse me. Where is Peter Pan?" a female tourist asked in halting English.

"Follow the water. You can't miss it." I gestured in the direction she should go.

The woman rejoined her group, three adults and five kids, presumably supplying the directions in her native language.

"Look at you. The Peter Pan pro."

"Soon, I'll be leading tours." I blew on my fingertips and brushed them against the front of my shirt.

"That right there is how you're so very American. Once, I was put on the spot at work and only learned I'd be leading a meeting five minutes prior to said meeting. I thought to myself: *Just be American*!"

"Did it work?"

"Unfortunately, too well. Now, I always lead the Wednesday morning meetings."

"Oh, no." I couldn't help it and ended up laughing.

"The good news is I also got a raise."

"You see! It's not so bad."

She squeezed my hand.

A squirrel ran across the path.

"Hey, Earl."

The squirrel climbed a tree, disappearing on the other side.

"You really do name everything." She tugged on my hand. "What's your name for your hair dryer?"

"Truvy Jones."

"Did you just come up with that?"

"Yep." I smacked my lips. "That's the name of Dolly Parton's character in *Steel Magnolias*. I love that movie."

"Haven't seen it."

I stopped in my tracks. "This is getting out of hand. You haven't seen any of my favorite movies. Not one!" Then something to my left caught my eye. "Look at that." I pointed across the grass.

Imogen shielded her eyes from the sun. "What?"

"The palace."

She seemed to understand. "It's going to take some getting used to for you, I think."

"It really is. We should have a picnic here sometime."

"I'd like that."

"It's so weird to me, wandering a park with a palace in the distance. Why am I allowed here? Or you?"

"I thought nothing stopped Americans from taking land that doesn't belong to them."

"Zinger!" I licked my finger and made a mark in the air.

She bobbed her head side to side, implying the slam was a layup. "This land used to be private. Henry the Eighth liked to hunt—"

"Not Earl the Squirrel's ancestors!" I playfully interjected.

"Deer, I think. If memory serves, it was still closed to the public in the eighteenth century, but over time that loosened. At first, you had to be respectably dressed, but—" She motioned to the many sun worshippers in shorts and tanks, some even in bikinis. "If you like strolling here, I think you'll really like Holland Park. That's near me. I usually run there on the weekends."

"Not this weekend," I teased.

"Some woman has been monopolizing my time."

"She sounds rude."

"You'd think so, but she really isn't. In fact, I find her fascinating, funny, and charming."

"Is she a keeper, then?"

Imogen gazed into my eyes. Making eye contact was one of her sexy strengths. "We'll see."

"If this is going to work, I'm going to have to introduce you to the right kind of movies."

"I could say the same for you, you know."

"Always willing to try something new."

"It's one of your endearing qualities." She stopped at a fork in the path. "If we go that way"—she pointed to the left—"I think we'll end up on Queensway. There's an M&S there."

"What's that?"

"A store where I can buy clean knickers and a shirt for dinner."

"You could always go commando, and you look adorbs in my Red Sox shirt." I arched one eyebrow.

"Commando in jeans? I don't know about you Americans, but I'm quite fond of my bits."

"Good point. I'm becoming quite fond of your bits and the rest of you."

We veered away from the water. "I wish this day would last forever."

"Time is cruel sometimes."

"It can be. Speaking of time, I may need a couple of extra days to finish reading *Where the Crawdads Sing*. I didn't get past page one last night. Like you, I've been distracted by a woman."

"What's with these women interrupting our lives?"

She laughed with me, our fingers interlacing once again, like they were fated to do so, and that thought didn't terrify but comforted me.

"I think I was always meant to move here."

"Why's that?" she asked.

"It's a feeling I can't shake," I said, while I thought: *To find you.*

EPILOGUE

After tapping my Oyster card, I rushed through the stampede at St. Paul's tube station, opting to walk down on the left side of the escalator, having to dodge the odd tourist (daily commuters knew the drill) who didn't properly stand on the right to let those in a hurry pass.

When I got to the bottom, I headed for the Central Line to catch a train to Lancaster Gate. Luckily, there was a train with the doors still open. Unfortunately, it was packed. Even that didn't deter me. I made room by pushing my way in, once again having to finagle around tourists, who insisted on standing at the entrance instead of moving into the train.

Part of me understood their hesitation, unsure of the stops and protocol. The other part of me wanted to explain to them in my brash American manner to get the fuck out of the way. They weren't the only people on the planet, jeez!

Imogen would probably point out that logic applied to me as well. She loved to poke holes in my Americanness. I did the same when she was being super British, like only placing one thinly sliced piece of ham on a sandwich. One! And, if you held it up, you could see through it.

At the next station, after some people got off the train, I moved farther in to get some breathing room. The following stop, Holborn, would leave the train half empty since it was only after two in the afternoon and it was the best option for the British Museum.

Sure enough, I scored a seat and read a paperback for the remaining five stops, getting off at Lancaster Gate. Again, I rushed, taking the winding stairs instead of waiting for the elevator.

Once I was back out in the sunshine, I sucked in the summer air, peering up into the vast blue sky. To my left was Kensington Gardens, but I made my way to a pub on this side of Bayswater Road. Pulling my hat from my bag, I put it on to combat the blinding sun bouncing off windshields from the cars stuck in traffic.

The outdoor seating wasn't packed yet, but in another hour or so, there wouldn't be a table. Not on a beautiful Friday afternoon. I claimed a table in the shade by setting my book and bag down and headed inside to order two pints.

Nigel was chatting with a gentleman in the corner, and I gave a friendly wave.

He popped up out of the chair, surprisingly spry for a man in his seventies, and approached. "Rory, can I get you to change your mind?"

"It's not my mind that needs changing. The two-year lease is up, and my company won't continue to pay for the flat." Not to mention I was ready for a change, wanting a space bigger than a breadbox.

"But, you're the only one in the building I like. The Russian lady on the first floor is so demanding."

It wasn't the first time I'd heard about her, or the French man on the ground floor. For a man who loved to rail about immigrants, he had no issues taking foreigners' money.

"I'm sorry, Nigel. I am, but it's out of my hands." I squeezed his shoulder, and his gentleman friend pursed his lips.

"Uh-oh. I better get back." Nigel kissed both of my cheeks, his scruff rubbing uncomfortably against my skin.

"Two Camden Hells, please," I said to the bartender.

A pair of arms wrapped around my waist. "Come here often?"

I leaned against Imogen. "As much as I can."

"Will you miss it?"

I glanced toward Nigel, who was laughing with his friend, and then at the bartender pouring the second pint. Lastly, I looked over my shoulder at the park across the street. "I really will. Living in this neighborhood for the past two years has been amazing."

After I tapped my card, we carried the beers out to the table, taking our seats.

Imogen hoisted her drink into the air. "To the neighborhood."

I clinked my glass to hers. "I'm still mad you called this place a tourist trap in your pub book. It's one of my faves."

"I called it a charming tourist trap, though."

I snarled at her.

"How was work?" she asked, clearly trying to get me away from this conversation thread since it wasn't the first time I'd voiced my displeasure.

"My boss is upset I'm leaving for a three-week holiday."

Imogen nodded. "I imagine he is. He'll actually have to work, which is something he hasn't done much of since opening the London office."

Again, my eyes sought out the greenness beyond the wall of the garden. "He's your typical good old boy, who got the job because of his family connections, not hard work. He thinks tossing around words like *notional* in a meeting is the extent of what he needs to do to succeed. What about you?"

"Sadly, I have to work for a living and have never used the word notional." She grinned.

"Trust me; it's one of your selling points." I

waggled my brow in what I hoped conveyed one of many of her positives. "Seriously, how was your day?"

"Time passed so slowly. Why does that happen when counting down the minutes?"

"I find it's best not to count minutes on your last day before heading out of the country for a once-in-a-lifetime adventure!"

"Now you tell me." She took another drink of her beer. "Are you packed?"

"Yep on both fronts. Luggage is ready to go, and my movers are arriving tomorrow. Do you know one of the guys who helped me move into the flat two summers ago is helping me this time around?"

"That can't be an easy job."

"Probably not, but he's still in his mid-twenties, and he says his wife likes his muscles."

"As opposed to us old folks."

"One foot in the grave." I extended a leg, pressing it down on the paving stone.

"My sister is all set with Clemmie. Finally, she gets to watch my baby to payback for all the times I've babysat my nephew."

"Luckily for us, she adores Clemmie."

"Taking the dog for a walk gets her out of the house and allows her mind to wander when she's stuck with a story."

Nigel and his friend ambled by, Nigel speaking loudly and animatedly.

"I'm actually going to miss the old curmudgeon."

"He has some good points," Imogen conceded. "He fixed the boiler as soon as it went out. Not a lot of landlords would have been so proactive."

"True." I leaned on my forearms. "What's my new landlady like?"

"You have a landlady this time?"

"Yep. You might know her. Blonde. Blue eyes. Droll sense of humor. Likes to read books." I flipped the pages of my paperback. "She's always recommending ones to me."

"She sounds boring." Imogen made a snoring sound.

"It's not entirely her fault. She's in the insurance biz."

"Oh, dear. She's gone from boring to dreadful." Imogen leaned on her forearms.

"It's okay. The accountant in me respects someone who crunches numbers."

My phone rang, and I whispered my boss's name. I answered on the fourth ring. "I'm officially on holiday, Adrian."

"I know, I know. But, can you walk me through the end of day reports again?"

I silenced a sigh, got up, and paced the sidewalk, constantly ducking tourists with rolling bags, while I talked him through it again. "On Monday, you won't be able to get a hold of me. I'll be in Africa."

"Does your place not have internet?"

I wish I could say he was teasing, but Adrian

wasn't the type to crack a joke. Not one that was funny. "Nope. Good luck."

In my absence, Imogen had gotten us a package of salt and vinegar crisps.

"Everything okay?" She bit into one.

"I'm cringing thinking about how many things I'll have to correct when we get back from Botswana." I sucked on a crisp, savoring the extra tanginess of the vinegar.

"Luckily for you, that's three blissful weeks away." She tapped the bill of my *Bedknobs and Broomsticks* hat.

I spread out my arms and sighed. "I can't believe we're actually going."

"That's not the only exciting part of your life, is it?"

"Everything about my life is exciting. I'm moving in with you. My company has hired me permanently for the London office. And, we're getting on a plane tomorrow night for Africa." I checked the date on my phone, even though it was basically seared into my memory bank. "Can you believe we met two years ago almost to the day?"

"Hasn't it been longer? It feels so much so."

"Says the woman who upended all of my plans, asking me to stay in London with her."

"You're the only person who likes to get buttermilk pancakes with me every Sunday." She flashed me her killer smile.

"Glad to know that's paid off for me. Because…" I leaned over the table.

She reciprocated, her face practically touching mine. "Because…?"

"I can't imagine my life without you."

"Luckily, you don't have to. Considering we're moving in together and going on our first wild adventure—"

"Finally!"

"Someone had to finish her original work contract and negotiate a new one." She hoisted her beer to her lips.

"I see how this relationship will be. You're going to blame me for everything?"

"You're the one who refused to move in a year ago when I asked you to."

"We fell for each other fast and hard. It seemed like the safe thing to do to make sure it wouldn't crash and burn. Besides, your family needed more time to get used to the fact that you didn't want to join them every single Saturday. Are they surviving only seeing you twice a month?"

"They still say, *See you next week!*"

I shook my head, chuckling, knowing it was true since I went with Imogen once a month, which was a lot of family time for the likes of me. "I can't say anything. My mom keeps saying she's going to visit, but then there's a work emergency."

"I didn't mind going to LA to meet her. Part of me

wonders if I was meant to live the Hollywood lifestyle."

That made me roar with laughter. "You've never driven a car. No way you can be a Californian."

"So, my California dream is dead?" she joked.

"Yes, darling. You know I can't live within a five-hour drive of my mom."

She lifted my hand to her lips and kissed my fingertips. "I blame you for that, as well."

"The kiss?"

"For making me fall for you, sacrificing so much."

"I'll gladly take the blame for the first. I'm easy to fall for. But I would like it noted, you came up with your family solution all on your own, not wanting to spend every Saturday for life with them."

"You Americans!" she huffed, clearly not wanting to talk about her family since it was still a work in progress. "Always full of yourselves."

"Shut up and kiss me for real this time."

"You're also bossy—"

I silenced her with my lips.

A HUGE THANK YOU!

First, thanks so much for reading *The Setup*. I've published more than twenty novels, and I still find it simply amazing people read my stories. When I hit publish on my first book back in 2013, I had no idea what would happen. It's been a wonderful journey, and I wouldn't be where I am today without your support.

If you enjoyed the story, I would really appreciate a review. Even short reviews help immensely.

Finally, don't forget if you want to stay in touch, sign up for my newsletter. I'll send you a free copy of *A Woman Lost*, book 1 in the A Woman Lost series, plus the bonus chapters that are exclusive to subscribers. And, you'll be able to enter monthly giveaways to win one of my books. Here's the link to join: http://eepurl.com/dtzNv1

ABOUT THE AUTHOR

TB Markinson is an American who's recently returned to the US after a seven-year stint in the UK and Ireland. When she isn't writing, she's traveling the world, watching sports on the telly, visiting pubs in New England, or reading. Not necessarily in that order.

Her novels have hit Amazon bestseller lists for lesbian fiction and lesbian romance. For a full listing of TB's novels, please visit her Amazon page.

Feel free to visit TB's website (lesbianromancesbytbm.com) to say hello. On the *Lesbians Who Write* weekly podcast, she and Clare Lydon dish about the good, the bad, and the ugly of writing. TB also runs I Heart Lesfic, a place for authors and fans of lesfic to come together to celebrate and chat about lesbian fiction.

Want to learn more about TB. Hop over to her *About* page on her website for the juicy bits. Okay, it won't be all that titillating, but you'll find out more.

Printed in Great Britain
by Amazon